Conclusions to Beginnings

Written and Illustrated by
Serella Savenko

Published by Cozy Nook Publishing LLC
CozyNookPublishing.com

Library of Congress Control Number: 2025942373

Source of Publication: Cozy Nook Publishing LLC, Hiram, GA USA
Date of Production: July 2025
Printed and bound in the United States.
Conclusions to Beginnings. 1st edition.

This book is dedicated, with love and gratitude,
to my family and friends who helped me along the way.

A special thanks to Elliot and Kira.

Everyday Adventure: Wildlings

Here is a normal tale of common events; it begins with Conclusions and finishes with Beginnings. It is boring; full of mundane things like unicorn guides, ideas orchards, mysterious knights, and marginalia. Being exceedingly ordinary, I don't recommend you read it. Best to skip it and try something more interesting.

Introductions

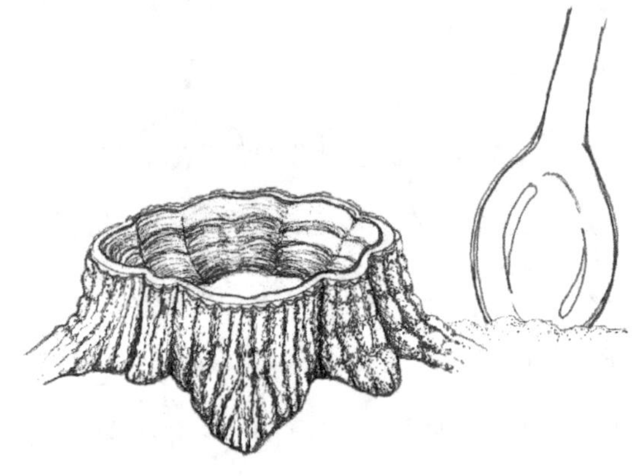

There are so many places to begin; so many stories to choose from, and paths to take. Some stories curl up, like a smooth snail shell, all polished and cozy; they are bigger than you might think, while also being safe and snug. And they are often pleasantly able to be enjoyed with a tasty treat and a favorite drink.

Let us begin on an ordinary path of soil and stone, through an ordinary garden of bushes, up to the door of an ordinary house. Well, perfectly ordinary for where it is.

In the garden, the brilliant sunlight glints on metal as the Mighty Teaspoon Hammer crashes down onto the Maplestump Mortar. A resounding CRACK rends the air. In a puff of pulverized dust, the last of the oats and beech nuts are vanquished, ground up fine.

The wielder of the Mighty Teaspoon Hammer is a gnome of tea, named Tonic Cuppa.

Tonic lives in a ceramic teapot house, with one cinnamon tree growing among the tea bushes out front, and a nicely tended tisane garden out back with pine, lemon, elder, sage, lavender, and many more good plants to steep.

Tonic and the house both waft of all things tea; the freshness of mint and orange, the warmth of nutmeg and clove, the uplifting of jasmine and peach blossoms, all swirled together. Along the garden path is a sturdy Maplestump Mortar. It is upon this mortar that Tonic uses the Mighty Teaspoon Hammer as a pestle to crush and powder nuts, bark, and other tough ingredients for tea. After being ground and mixed, the ingredients are stored in a variety of neatly-labeled tins until they are ready to sell, steep, and sip.

The ornate Passion Flower cauldron near the front door Tonic uses to brew delicate blends, and the sharp Chestnut Burr cauldron opposite it the gnome uses for tough, unruly blends. The blackberry bramble by the cauldrons watches over the garden. Gnome and Bramble have been best friends since they were both new.

Once the Maplestump Mortar is clean and the ingredients stored away inside the house, Tonic sits on a brightly colored cushion in the main room, finishing a morning cup of tea and buffing out dents in the Mighty Teaspoon Hammer. Glancing into the mug of finished tea, Tonic reads the pattern in the leaf dregs and perks up, just moments before the garden bell rings, "Friends arriving! Thanks, tea leaves!" the gnome says brightly.

With sunlight pouring in through the saucer-shaped windows, the gnome's house is steeped in light. Racing first into the ceramic kitchen while muttering, "Tea cups! Vaccinium tea cups... the cranberry? No, I think we will use blueberry today," and then walking carefully to the door with the filled tea cups balanced on a wooden tray. Tonic's brown hair puffs and their leafy-green tips seem to glow in the sun, and the light causes dirt smudges and tea stains to show like merit badges on the gnome's sturdy brown and green overalls and the outfit's brightly stitched leaf patterns.

Tonic cheerfully declares in a rush, "Greetings and Hospitality!" while opening the green walnut-hull door of the house and walking out with three cups to offer the waiting friends a, "fresh, cold cup of Rosehip-Violet-Mallow tea for you! I made this blend for Port Manteau, to help the sailors stay healthy and keep away scurvy. What do you think?!" The gnome swishes side to side while awaiting the friends' reactions.

A small pooka with spiky black hair buzzes up to Tonic first. Putting an oakcorn basket down on the garden table, Clover Miel sips the offered tea and dances with delight. The pooka's hands leap and twirl "What a sweet concoction; I shall have to bring some back to the Bloomiery and Apis Distillery! I would like to trade a heaping Spoonful of this blend for some of our newest batch of honey." Clover indicates the oakcorn basket (some might say 'acorn,' but as they come from oak trees, not ac trees, 'oakcorn' only makes sense) on the garden table, then adds with a confident flourish of fingers, "Today's honey is a fresh flavor, made from blueberry, apricot, and thyme flowers." The two friends agree to trade a large tin of tea for an oakcorn of honey.

While Tonic is handing Clover a teacup, the coblyn standing next to the stone bench ties back long, citrine hair with a willow reed and grape vine. While the tresses are tied back, shimmery opal hues glimmer within the hair. Then Tonic passes over a cup of the iced tea and the coblyn's grey-green eyes brim with curiosity from behind large, round, gem-studded goggles with smokey quartz lenses. Taking a big sip, Facet Cabichon makes a chirrup of delight, and hums so happily that some tea sloshes! With amethyst vest and amber shirt now slightly-soaked with tea, the coblyn quickly pulls out an extra cloth from one of many pockets on the complex belt (which is full of tools for making jewelry, gadgets for fixing gears, and several Possibility Parts). While mopping up the spill, Facet asks "What makes the blend so refreshing? It tastes like a sunlit cave full of glistening gems!"

As the tea gnome explains about types of tea and floral flavors, Facet takes out a well-worn birchbark journal (coblyns highly prize these birch bark journals, because they keep the ideas inside fresh) and writes down notes, including the question "Camellia sinensis; what makes white, green, and black tea?" Then Facet discovers a Sudden Idea about travel while sketching a new tea-strainer design. Coblyns often keep Sudden Ideas as pets; some Sudden Ideas even transform into Useful Creations and do heaps of good in the world. Sudden Ideas must be fed with research, exercised with practice, and given lots of attention. These cute critters *might* look like just about anything, but what they tend to look like is a really fancy beetle. They always have a beetle's hard wing case, which is usually patterned to match what Idea they are about, and they are most easily seen and identified by coblyns and other creators. When Facet spots a Sudden Idea, the coblyn pulls on goggles made of metal and gems to better study the creature. These goggles have smokey quartz lenses to reduce glare, fur trim to trap distractions, and multiple gems for as-yet-unknown reasons. The goggles are useful for when days are too bright as well.

Lastly, Tonic hands the third cup of tea to the water sprite, who is happily splashing in the stream which winds through the handle-side of the garden. The splashing has watered the closest portion of garden and dampened the sprite's fluttery clothes, turning light grey to deep blue, and highlighting the rainbow shimmers. Briny Nimbus accepts the tea from Tonic and swishes the delicate cup joyfully in hands that are the light creamy-white color of frothy waves, before gulping the tea down. An ever-present breeze ruffles the sprite's short, wavy hair, making the ends foam and curl like ocean surf. Offering the last bit of tea in the flower-shaped cup to the whirling wind, Briny's smile shines. "A delicious blend, Tonic. Thank you!"

With a hiccupping buzz, Clover exclaims, "Oh, the time!" The pooka puts down a now-empty tea cup, and zips around for three brief hugs, then grabs the large tin of tea in both hands and zooms away down the path. At the main road, Clover clambers into a carriage decorated with bright yellow and cool grey geometric patterns. With a whistle, the pooka starts the yellow and grey carriage with a jounce, and bounces off, looking like the largest bumbling bee ever. The pooka's rich voice echoes back to the teapot, "Sorry I cannot stay; I've got to fly back to the Bloomiery or the Marzipandas will be ravenous! Well met, and meet again!"

The three remaining friends enjoy time in Tonic's garden sipping tea, tasting honey, and discussing their upcoming Craft Course Conclusions. The sun shines brightly, and the day is warm, a welcome notice of Summer approaching. The frost is gone, and gardenias have started to bloom. The friends bask in the sunlight that lazily dapples the garden through the tea leaves and enjoy watching the cool breeze that always floats around Briny. While quietly relaxing, each friend considers the upcoming Conclusion Day, only a season away.

Tonic worries: Am I good enough? Strong enough? I feel so stagnant, sometimes. I want to grow! Can I brew and smash and blend the way they want? What if I have to grow a plant? That takes me ages… Will anyone like my tea?

Briny frets, flipping frothing locks of seafoam away: Who will I be? Conclusions determine our work and our future. We chose our Craft Courses, and our future is firm. Will I wither without Weather? Can Tides truly turn a task terrible? Conclusions are the Culmination of our curricular career! Oh,

I'm so scared I'm ailing with alliterations..."

Facet sketches furiously, channeling nervousness into productivity: Am I inspiring enough? How many nibs will I break on my pens? Do I have the charisma to influence others? Does anyone really enjoy my art? What if my mechanics are all wrong? Will I trip and spill and break everything?

After this thought-filled pause Briny pipes up, "Is it really, though? I mean... I was just thinking about our upcoming Conclusions. And, well, they always seem so important. I just wondered if they are, really? We get evaluated on our skill in the crafts we chose to take, that is true. But do the Conclusions actually determine who we are? Do they dictate what we do, or set our worth? What if I want to change crafts after my Conclusion?!"

Facet encourages the friends with a smiling insight, "Conclusions hinge on one professor's perception, on one stressful day. As tests, the Conclusions seem so big and important, and very scary. The Conclusions we get give us a boost in that career. But really, Briny is right. They aren't all we can do. We will do our best, and no matter what our Conclusions turn out to be, we will still be exactly who we are."

Feeling better, Tonic leads the trio inside the cool teapot abode, adding on to Facet's explanation, "Did you know that Clover never took a Craft Course or Conclusion? Clover is great! The honey from the Apis Distillery wouldn't be half as good if Clover weren't there. That pooka knows honey flavor!" Briny and Facet agree, while enjoying the gnome's hospitality, and assisting with kitchen clean-up.

Dusting speckled, moss-bark hands together after washing up the dishes, Tonic thoughtfully asks the friends, "How would you like to help the world? Or maybe the question is: what are your favorite skills?"

Briny's answer is breezy, "The water is my passion. I would like to work with tide and current traffic schedules. And I could have a little tidal pool farm, where I would keep a fluffle of windrabbits. Have you ever seen the Sea Bunny breeds? So cute! Of course, it might be interesting to work with my cousin on Storm Runs too."

Tonic leans against the curve of the ceramic kitchen, and nods pensively, lost in thought.

After a moment of fidgeting, Facet answers with an avalanche of words, "I love working with metals and stones! It is so satisfying to find a fascinating stone, research it, learn about it, polish it, and combine it with a beautiful metal to create useful jewelry! Did you know I'm researching how to make a Stratigraphy Skirt too? Beauty and expression are so subjective and definitive of who we are; I want to create things that are expressive and functional. Of course, I enjoy inventing and tinkering with gears too. I wonder if I could make beautiful, wearable items with metal and stones and moving gears? Ohhh, what if..." and here Facet's words tumble to a halt as the birchbark journal is brought out again. The coblyn adjusts the smokey goggles and scribbles quickly, to capture some questions and thoughts on paper.

Briny and Tonic walk back outside smiling, as Facet drifts along behind, still sketching, and following them by peripheral vision.

Some cloud-cover makes the weather brisk as the trio explore the streambank, and Tonic asks, "Do you ever wonder what other places are like? Do you think there could be different jobs and needs in other places? I've just...never really gone very far from my teapot and garden."

With the wave of a hand, Briny rushes to answer. "Of *course* other places have different jobs and needs! You could hardly be a successful Sand Caster on the ice floes of the Oblivion Sea; every place has its own resources. Of course, everywhere has *some* kind of weather. I would probably travel a *lot* if I worked Storm Runs! But even then, different climates would mean different types of weather work."

Facet finishes jotting down a rambling trail of notes and inspirations, and looks around. The goggles go back on, as the coblyn squints at the daylight; "Oh. Are we outside, then?"

Laughter pours out of Tonic and the heavy thoughts of crafts, Conclusions, and distant places float away. Sprite and coblyn join right in, and the three friends laugh and forget their worries for a bit. It is as soothing as a good cup of tea, a rainy day, or an interesting puzzle. The friend chat and play happily for the rest of the lovely, late Spring afternoon. The Conclusions still loom large, but their looming seems a little less ominous with the support of friends. Still, the trio will face their Conclusions one day, and sooner than they might want.

Chapter 1: Craft Conclusions

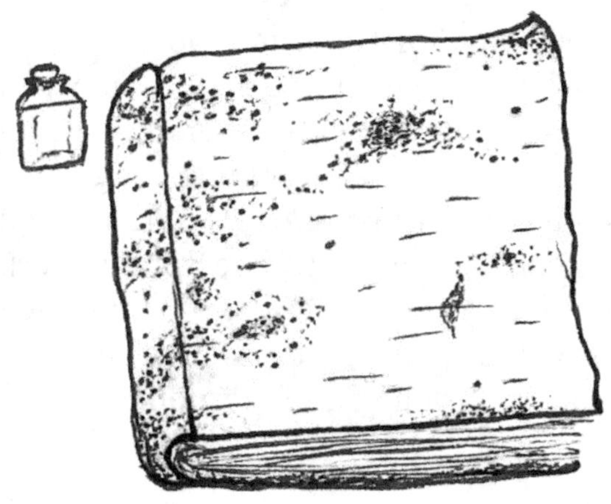

The Wheel of the Year turns. Spring has slipped into Summer, and thoughts of Autumn loom crisp and crunchy on the distant horizon. Facet, Briny, and Tonic visit together regularly to study and practice their skills. Clover often stops by to share stories and help, between work duties at the Bloomiery and Apis Distillery. While the friends study for their Craft Courses, and try not to fret or worry, while they practice and talk through the day, and do their best to support each other. Summer seems warmer this year, taking its time to bring the crisp, cozy weather of Autumn; lizards lie about, soaking in the lingering heat. Plants wilt instead of getting ready to rest, and Tonic uses the Mighty Teaspoon Hammer to dig up several overheated plants, relocating them closer to water and shadier spots. To take their minds off of the unexpected heat, the friends take turns focusing on each other's interests, and offer encouragement; sometimes they tend to Tonic's gardens, or spin dandelion thread for Briny's windsocks, or dig up window stones with Facet. Always they share whimsies, silences, and ideas.

One such early Autumn day, still bright and sticky-warm, all three friends are at Facet's house. The coblyn has a little house cut into a hill, a tidy cave. The windows and skylights are colored jewels, and the kitchen glows with the comfort of iron kettles and copper pots and ladles. The floor is hard packed dirt and stone, and all the bowls are earthenware. There is metal and stone in every part of the house, which Facet says gives a solid grounding of thought. Although the hillside roof is hot, inside the cave is refreshingly cool.

While they practice skills and help each other rehearse facts for the Conclusions, Tonic speaks up. "I was thinking today about how many tea flavors are out there, and that led me to thinking about the world, and how much Graemes travels, and how many teas I've never even sniffed or sipped! I miss Graemes coming to visit and telling stories. And… maybe I want an adventure of my own? A chance to really branch out and explore!" Tonic rushes to explain, "I want to find Graemes. I want to go learn new things! I just feel… stuffy, and fussy, and like everything is just… the *same*. Everyday. I feel stuck. I want to go find Graemes, so that I'm doing something new!"

Briny's breeze blows anxiously, gusting around the scent of sea salt and ozone like a tidal wave. "We haven't even completed Professor Tome's course yet; you know Tome gets cross when anybeing leaves a Craft Course early!" With wide, worried eyes, Briny knits little dust whorls in the air.

Tonic agrees, in a hesitant way, "…You are right. We need to finish our Craft Courses, and do our best on our Conclusions. I know they aren't far off now. Whatever the Conclusions might mean to us, we started with this training and we should finish it." The gnome idly crushes stray seeds with sullen smacks of the Mighty Teaspoon Hammer.

Facet adds the encouragement, "Then we can decide what to do from there, after Conclusions are completed! Once we have our Conclusions, we can choose to do *anything*."

Over the course of days, and in between courses, the friends continue to study and practice. They fall into a comfortable routine as the days slide, slowly, languidly, toward crispness, and Conclusion rush swiftly toward them. Craft Conclusion studies become the friends' sole focus. Some days they study quietly, some days are loud with games of Quiz Catch.

And then:

It is Conclusion day, and Tonic wakes, slowly unfurling limbs. "Time to break our fast!," the gnome calls out the window to Bramble. Sleepily sipping tea, Tonic takes a cooled cupful out to the blackberry bush by the door, to share the breaking of the nightime fast. In the tea garden, Tonic ensures all the plants have plenty of compost and clean water; normally it would be time to put down a warm layer of woodchips too, but the warm weather means the plants are ready to snuggle up yet. The heat of summer hangs on, and Tonic wonders if there is a better way to cool down the garden. The gnome sings and talks while working in the garden, tending every plant. Once done, Tonic grabs the peach pack from the door, swiftly shoves in some supplies, belatedly remembers to brush the garden dirt off, and heads to Professor Tome's Conclusion.

It is Conclusion Day, and Facet wakes with a creak and a groan. The coblyn sits bolt upright when a Sudden Idea flies in and lands squarely on the bed. Facet pets the fleeting Idea's brilliant blue wings, then feeds it a sketch and a notion. Dressing in a favorite set of bismuth-hued brogues, Facet bounds to the door. Then the coblyn corkscrews and comes right back in to grab the bronze bag from the bed. Turning several more times, Facet finally remembers to oil the door hinges, bring the birchbark journal along, and break the morning fast with a tasty, chilled stone soup.

It is Conclusion Day, and Briny wakes in a fluttering mood, pushing off waves of sheets. The sprite has a little sandcastle home in a shipwreck that has been pulled up halfway onto land in a sandy cove. The walls are made of bits of the ship's hull, and where there is only "wreck" and no "ship" the walls are a sand, glass, and seashell mixture called tabby; there are windows and skylights in abundance, and it is very tidy. The sprite doesn't keep or collect very many things; new items arrive on the tide to be decorations for a day or two, then are washed away again into the sea. This location is the perfect spot for tidal activities, as well as windrabbit training. The house is decorated with shells and has a lovely kelp-thatching roof. Spinners, windsocks, and chimes adorn the mast and porch. The underwater portion of the sandcastle is filled with clams and crabs and fishes, and has a perpetual bubble current for carpeting. On Conclusion day, the air is humid as the sprite feeds tiny leaves to Spindrift, the ever-present breeze, as it ruffles curtains and blows foam sculptures around the room. Next, Briny washes tangled waves of hair, checks on the clouds above the cove, and quickly cleans up a messy current just outside the shipwreck's hull. After breaking sleep's fast with a bowl of beautifully brined bubbles and grabbing the seafoam satchel, Briny rushes out the door trailing a wake of confidence.

The friends aren't able to meet up before their Conclusions. Each enters a different Craft Course area, to face different tests and challenges. So a dizzying forever later, after Conclusions have concluded, Facet and Briny wait outside for Tonic, trading tales of their day.

"Clover was in the Cluster judging my Conclusion." Facet

goes on, "They always need more coblyn builders at the Bloomiery. There's so much honeycomb to build, flowers to tend, and amber gems to shape, plus pollen distribution, and the hive works! Clover offered me work there at the Bloomiery. Did you know I had to build two Devices, while timed, over a volcano fissure? And they didn't provide me with any Promising Possibilities! Fortunately, I had brought a Sudden Idea in my birchbark, and it worked perfectly. Alloy even asked to keep it – said they could raise it and use it near the Trellis. My final Conclusion was Builder with Strong Inventing. Or was it Inventor with Strong Building? The point is, I'm as stoked as a roaring fire!"

Briny is ebullient too, describing in detail the harrowing tasks with sea-serpents, full moon, riptides, and a bleaching coral. "With Rivulets and riptides everywhere! But I tamed the sea-serpent and managed to get the Whirlpools back into the pen. Of course, it helped to have Spindrift with me. I was docked points for leaving my tasks to untangle a young kelpie caught in seaweed; Professor Woolen gave me extra marks, though, for a Storm Empath. I still have scratches where the sea-serpent thrashed me during its tantrum; look! I'm happy as harp seals that the serpent's temper finally blew over. My Tally took some time, and I was afraid I had washed out..." Then Briny gushes, "My Conclusion was Weather with Strong Tidal Tendencies!"

Many more students leave, in various states of excitement, sobriety, and some even nursing wounds. When Briny and Facet finally find Tonic sitting in a gloomy sadness on a bench, they are worried about their wilted friend.

"My Conclusion was inconclusive." Tonic mopes with a glowering frown. "Professor Tome said I would need to stay after to talk, after everyone was done." Tonic's green puffs are tattered, but the gnome stirs up some courage and asks, "How did you two do?"

As Briny and Facet start answer, Professor Tome calls Tonic over to speak. Coblyn and sprite are anxious for their friend, but wait patiently while the professor is speaking.

When the professor walks away, Tonic bubbles at the waiting friends, "I've been Concluded a Steeper! I can officially do Teawork, and was given an application for the Samovar!" Tonic's expression turns bitter as orange peel while continuing, "They noted my knowledge and curiosity, but wrote down 'Wildling' with *distaste*. I don't know what that means, but it didn't seem good. I mean, the only 'wildlings' I've ever hear of are ancient myths, heroes or tricksters on adventures to the World of Myth. I don't think I'm about to be a hero in some fictional story, popping into Mythwold! Why would they be upset about *myths*? I'm not even a storyteller!" After pausing in recollection, Tonic huffs and continues grumbling, "It was odd, but I think it was a tatty old book that bothered them most. When I grabbed my peach pack, a scruffy book fell out of it, and that was when the panel wrote "wildling" in my Conclusion. They said I might 'be a risk' so I'm not allowed to travel for three full moons. The book didn't seem to be anything special; it was just an old thing Graemes left at my house. I must have grabbed it by accident this morning."

Facet tries to direct focus on the good and exclaims "I'm so excited to know your blends will soon be in all the Tea Houses. And an application to the Samovar?! Exclusive! I will construct a gadget to move mountains just to visit you at the Samovar."

Briny joins in with a gusty sigh "I want to see your tea designs for the Samovar! Do you think the Samovar really requires special Clickfish to serve the tea in different bubbles of fresh or salt water?"

Cheering up from the friends' enthusiasm, Tonic's mood visibly lifts. The three friends celebrate their successes at

Raincakes bakery with candied kelp and dancing and singing silly songs, and cheering each other on. While celebrating, Tonic holds high some kelp, and cheers "To Conclusions and new beginnings!" and the friends all heartily applaud. The trio joke and tell stories of their Conclusions, reenacting their favorite scenes. In the middle of a bite Facet laughs and snorts a morsel of cake, and consequently coughs, sneezes, and causes much concern. The friends pat the coblyn's back, grab handkerchiefs, offer water to drink, accidentally knock over a chair, and generally try to help. With eyes still watering, but mostly recovered, Facet laughingly declares the experiment a success: they discovered that cake is still not breathable. Facet, Tonic, and Briny decide they have all had enough science and festivity for one day, and head home in bright moods.

The sprite, coblyn, and gnome live their lives and forget about finding Graemes for a while. Facet visits the Bloomiery, and works on Building skills. Tonic tends the tea gardens, and sends in the application to the Samovar. Briny studies up on Tides, and trains the breezes that always blow around the lake. Grand Plans and Wild Ideas melt away into comfortable, mundane tasks. And our story could end here: the Marzipandas get fed honey and almonds, the tea plants get harvested, gears get cut, tides turn, and the friends live regular lives.

But, one day, as Tonic crushes up some particularly recalcitrant Anise seeds, something different happens.

Chapter 2: Curious Rituals

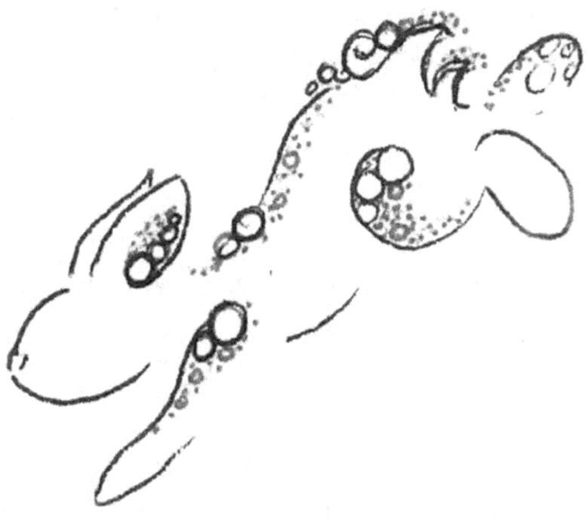

The Mighty Teaspoon Hammer shimmers in the sunlight, and with a groaning HEAVE Tonic sends the Teaspoon SMASHING down into the Maplestump Mortar. With a *smash, smack, crash, crack!* the seeds on the mortar become a fine powder and are then scooped up and added to the bowlful of black pepper and licorice root. Although it is now firmly Autumn and the days should have cooled, the heat of summer still lingers and today it *sizzles*; the chirping and clicking of birds and bugs buzzes lazily in the afternoon heat.

As Tonic clears away the debris from the Maplestump Mortar, Facet comes down the path at a quick click, huffing and puffing "I brought a Piece!"

Briny, too, hollers exhilaration at Tonic, speeding up the stream with arms windmilling through the water, "The collars are done!"

Cheering "Greetings and Hospitality, everybeing!" in both directions, the gnome waits for either friend to make sense, with one hand on a hip and the other supporting the Mighty Teaspoon Hammer.

Facet explains that the Piece was found while following a Sudden Idea, "and Pieces become ever so useful if there's a Bit to go with them!"

Tonic grins with surprise "I found a Bit hiding in the house just this morning! I would never have spotted it if you hadn't taught me how. You will need to go find it though, Facet; it hid before I could hiccup, somewhere in the bookshelves."

Briny gushes with enthusiasm "I completed the mist collars I was making and caught you each a windrabbit!" The sprite pulls out a twitching, kicking seafoam satchel full of boisterous air to show the friends. The satchel appears empty, but is jerking and bulging as though full of something eager to get out. Tonic's orange eyes go saucer-round with delight "That's amazing, Briny! I've never actually seen a windrabbit, although you have mentioned them often."

The sprite replies, "I thought about Sea Bunnies because they are smaller, but windrabbits are easier to care for. Tonic, help me make a safe area to let them roam in your garden."

While Tonic and Briny make space for the windrabbits outside, Facet goes inside and catches the aforementioned Bit with ease, finding it on top of a book in Tonic's teapot home. As the coblyn brings out the Bit on the book, Briny proudly displays two thin loops from the otherwise empty satchel. "I made one for each of us" the sprite explains, "they help you form a bond with your windrabbit by allowing you to see them! Otherwise the windrabbits are as invisible to you as a bluster."

Briny scoops a loop out of the air, and for the first time Tonic and Facet notice a small rabbit, shimmering like the reflection of wind and bouncing like bubbles, racing around

Briny; the rabbit jumps and turns around the sprite, kicking up air and splashing flecks of water from the sprite's hair. It is the perpetual gust that is always around Briny!

"This is my Spindrift. A beautiful Gale, and a really lucky wind for me." Briny states while petting the rambunctious rabbit. Next, Briny hands a bundle of air to Facet. Once Briny puts the collar on, it coalesces into a rabbit-shaped shifting, sparkling, mineral mist. Looking at the braided-metal collar, the coblyn reads the word 'Turbine' engraved on a gear pendant.

"I caught you each a Zephyr. They are a playful, friendly breed of windrabbit." Briny proudly pronounces.

With a joyful laugh, Tonic accepts the other fistful of twisting turbulence. Looking at the ceramic collar on the lagomorph materializing of sweetly-scented curling vapor, Tonic says "Hello, Steam! Tomorrow I'm going to make you a tiny teapot to rest in."

Facet sneezes suddenly, and Turbine bolts around, rattling windows and turning cartwheels. Steam escapes as well, adding a susurrus to the ruckus. Spindrift joins in, and the windrabbits tumble playfully around the garden, kicking up dry and wilted brush, and knocking over the book which tumbles the Bit that then falls in a heap in the pages.

The book is called Curious Rituals of Uncommon Folk, and it is written by Graemes.

Chapter 3: Wanderlustre

A large, hardy, well-read, and rather worn book full of writing and illustrations sits in front of the friends. They look over the fascinating volume and marvel at the intermittent illustrations. The book has a solid binding, rippled pages, and many tears, stains, and smudges. The cover is a tousled leather; 'foxed' might be a better description, as it smells slightly musky, too. There is, however, a pleasant hint of vanilla and lotus under the mustiness, and the numerous stains and scratches in the leather suggest many interesting adventures in the book's past. A small squirrel charm dangling at the end of a leather cord secures the book's closure.

"I think this is the book that fell out of my bag at my Conclusion." Tonic notes. Flipping through the pages, the gnome sounds bewildered, "It's Graemes's book! I didn't know Graemes wrote a book. I've seen the book on the shelf where Graemes always shoves stuff, but I never bothered to read it. It's ...a story about traveling? I think. Or maybe bedtime myths for youngbeings."

Facet quickly grabs the Bit as it dangles from a page and secures it in a vest pouch. Briny points to a place in the book where the Bit was and asks, quite puzzled, "What things are the World's Between?"

Finding the spot in the book that the sprite is looking at, Tonic reads it and then clarifies "Graemes says the World's Between are the places where overlapping worlds connect. It is the 'between' space of the worlds, like a doorway. Graemes describes the World's Between as... well, there is only so much space... I mean" Tonic falters, then tries again with a nose-wrinkle, "There is a lot of space Universe-wise, but the magic of life tends to cause clusters of reality. So where you have one world with enough magic for life, you get multiple realities overlapping."

Noticing the friends' confused expressions, Tonic continues "It is rather like when I put leaves in a big, open teapot." The gnome opens the sourwood teapot on the table, and swirls the water and leaves inside by way of example. "There is plenty of water for the leaves to all spread out. But the leaves tend to cluster together" Tonic points to the settling sediment "they group up in the best spaces for tea leaves to be. And the universe is like that too!" Tonic continues enthusiastically. "The universe is like one big teapot, and the magic which supports life and experiences settles like clusters of tea leaves! I think Graemes is saying Mythwold, the World of Myth, is real."

Beaming at the demonstration, the gnome goes on. "Since there isn't room in one world (or section of teapot) for all of the realities (or tea-clusters) that settle there, the possibilities overlap, and the World's Between is how you get from one reality to another." Proud of the metaphor, Tonic asks "Does that make sense?"

Briny and Facet think it over, exchanging looks. Turbine noses open Facet's pocket and pokes at the Bit.

"Not really" Briny admits, with an apologetic shrug.

"But we are glad you understand it!" Facet enthuses.

With a nose-wrinkle, Tonic looks at the book again. Reading quickly while flipping leaves furiously, the gnome motions to the journal between them all, "It seems that Graemes wrote this tome while traveling, and it describes the World's Between, an astonishing array of folk, Wildlings, and the World of Myth."

Briny's eyes flash "Wait! 'Wildlings' again? Wasn't that what upset your panel during your Conclusion?"

Facet nods in surprise, with coppery-patina eyes shining, while taking the Bit back from Turbine, and tucking it securely into a belt pocket.

Tonic agrees thoughtfully, "Yes, that's right. I think this book is just what I need. Remember when I was thinking about how much Graemes has traveled? How I wanted an adventure? But I put that aside to finish Craft Conclusions, and then there was so much to do after, that I sort of forgot. Maybe it's time to try again. Who remembers the last time Graemes visited? And no one even knows exactly where Graemes's most recent adventure *is*. I think this book is the catalyst to help find our missing mentor."

Invigorated by this new purpose, sprite, coblyn, and gnome look over Graemes's book, trying to decipher the point of it all. It is long and wandering at points, extremely abrupt at others. People are mentioned once, and then forgotten, others mentioned several times. There are occasional dates and landmarks jotted down, but no real chapters, nor cohesive storyline; no moral or lesson evident in it. And *many* areas are muddy, wrinkled, torn, stained, and otherwise indecipherable. The friends peruse the book, pausing at any phrases or illustrations that catch their attention, and slowly they discover a kind of story to it all, a story about lives and experiences.

After some time, Tonic picks up the previous thought, "This book is Graeme's story... or, really, a journal of Graeme's life. Life, story, they might be the same thing." Tonic's voice fills with a mix of respect and longing. "Graemes has met and spent time with a lot of people while traveling, and written the stories down! I think all of these stories mean, 'I am here. They are here.' I think that in the telling of life stories, Graemes illustrates that we all have stories; our lives are all stories to ourselves."

Tonic pauses, and Facet and Briny watch their friend, who clearly has some big thoughts to express. Tonic gulps a breath and rushes on, "We all have stories, but mine is just, 'gnome has a garden.' I feel like my story hasn't gone anywhere! What have I learned? What narrative do I have? I take my Craft Courses, I tend my garden, I use my Mighty Teaspoon Hammer to scoop, smash, and stir. I'm a good little gnome doing nothing much. ...I want to meet some of the people written about in the journal, and learn more stories! I want to travel and learn curious rituals and visit with uncommon folk like Graemes! I want to have experiences that make a better story and grow my self."

Briny shifts uncomfortably, tugging a strand of waving curls, but waits for the gnome to finish. Spindrift flits and rolls and kicks up clouds.

"I love my house, and my friends, my gardens, and my work." Tonic goes on, "But I also want to experience what else is out there! Graemes has traveled so much, and I still live where I always have. Maybe it is time I go wander, go learn new things, meet strange situations. Graemes always said 'Travel changes you' and I want to grow and change! I think it's time to go outside my comfortable and known."

Facet and Briny look at each other in surprise, then Briny's stormy eyes look hard at the gnome. "That sounds like more than a little Coddiwomple walk, that sounds like a Wanderlust." The sprite's blue-grey hair ripples and froths with concern. "You *just* finished your Conclusion and found your Craft! Don't you want to blend? You could create teas for the Samovar or the Curatives. Reading a book is one thing, a whole Wanderlust adventure is another thing."

Facet's feet shift uneasily and send the full-belt jangling. "Remember those questions you asked us over summer, before our Conclusions? About our passions and how we want to help the world? Your passion is tea. You want to help the world with healing blends and tasty steeping, don't you? Are you sure you want to leave just when you are about to start?" The coblyn frets, and crinkles a page of the birchbark journal, fingers sifting the pages like sand.

Tonic breathes in sharply and ponders, as Briny swirls in sharp circles.

Facet whispers "You can't ignore a Wanderlust, though. You would lose your Drive and Spark; you would grey to dust if you did."

Briny nods decisively. "That's true, Facet. A Wanderlust can't be ignored. Tonic, if you want to go, we support you. How can we help?"

Tonic's persimmon eyes glow with determination. "Your support means a lot! I would like to go together, if you are willing. What do we do for journey preparations?"

"We should gather knowledge, skills, and supplies," Facet states, thinking aloud and patting a multitude of pockets: "Let's bring Graemes's journal, for sure. We should take maps, and good boots and coats. I will groom my Sudden Ideas and look for Bits and Pieces. ...An extra pair of goggles. ...Oh, gears! And... is this a carnelian? Hm; no..." The coblyn continues muttering and exploring various pockets.

Briny swirls with excitement, causing grey sleeves to flutter and glimmer with iridescence in the light, and pipes up, "Yes, we will need to know where we are going and how to get there! Good thinking. We will also need snacks, and maybe a place to sleep on the journey; do you think we will get to camp out? I can train our windrabbits for communication, in case we get separated! And they can cool us and brace us along."

As Tonic starts to speak, a curious thing occurs.

A small air current stirs around the room, glittering lustrous in the sunlight, swirling against everyone, then bursting silently. Tonic stands up straight, patting both brown-green hair puffs nervously. "Well, that seems a propitious start to our adventure. A sort of sparkling *wanderlustre* to start us off! I hope it's helpful."

Looking around the garden, Tonic asks the blackberry plant, "Bramble, will you watch over the gardens? I don't know anyone who can care for them better!" The blackberry plant curls a tendril in the breeze. "Thank you." Tonic responds, while packing the Mighty Teaspoon Hammer for the trip.

All three friends positively fizz with energy, excited to go, though none of them yet know where.

Briny muses, "I know Clover has to keep working with the Marzipandas; that pooka will have no time for a Wanderlust! But, I bet Clover could check on Bramble while we're gone and help out with your garden. Clover does complain that the Bloomiery is very stationary work, and would probably enjoy a reason to ensure daily travel."

Facet breaks off a small willow twig and weaves a new hair tie. "It helps to have a companion or two on a journey, so I'm glad we three are going together.. Oohh! Briny, you mentioned sleep, which reminds me; we can take my new Contraption!" the coblyn giggles with delight "I built it using the Bits and Pieces I had; It's a Night Tent, and can convert into a boat! But also, it sometimes turns into a squashed sandwich."

The trio begin tidying, packing, and generally preparing for their journey. Briny sends Spindrift to deliver the request about Bramble to Clover. The friends part to ensure all is taken care of. Over the next two days, scones are baked, plants pruned, prunes planted, books organized, packs stuffed with packets and satchels packed with stuff, lists made, and 'to do's marked 'done.'

Two days later, the friends are together again in Tonic's tea garden, and Facet announces, "I already made a Scrubby Bubbleup to clean your cauldrons, Tonic, and I fixed a geode basin on the hill of my cave so that it would leak for the roaming Clickfish."

The friends discuss their packing work, and ensure everyone's homes are cared for, before deciding they are as prepared as they can be for the unknown. Tonic provides provisions, Facet is geared up with gears, and Briny watches the weather.

Looking at the seafoam satchel, peach pack, and bronze bag, Facet wonders "Well-packed is good, but then what? How do we start our adventure? Which direction do we go? We don't have any clues..." The coblyn fidgets, with a head full of worries, and finds it difficult to begin.

Facet pulls out a handful of coins, thinking they might need supplies while on their journey. The coblyn mutters, "Trades are preferred, but even though we can do tasks, it will be difficult to carry very much." Facet admires the coins: small, coppery and green-patina-ed Beans with a scalloped edge, silver Glamour coins etched with stars and smooth edges, and a few gold Pots carved with a cauldron on one side and a rainbow on the other. The coblyn smiles at the little metal coins as they pour into a pocket of the bronze bag.

Chapter 4: Snakeline

It is mid-morning, the friends have decided to start their Wanderlust journey this day, but Facet is fretting, "How do we start? If no one knows where Graemes is, then it is very difficult to begin our quest. Are there any clues in Graemes's Curious Rituals journal?"

Tonic swirls around, back toward the house. "Blooming rot; of course, Facet! I nearly forgot the book! People *do* know Graemes, and they might know where we need to go!" Cracking open the hickory hull door, the gnome rushes inside, Steam bobbing along behind. Before you can gulp, Tonic is bounding back into the garden, pouring over Curious Rituals of Uncommon Folk. "Here! I've been reading through the Curious Rituals of Uncommon Folk. Well, trying to, certainly; many areas are too smudged, torn, and worn for me to read. Graemes seems to have used anything at hand to write, and not all the inks were very steadfast, either." Briny peers at the book and Facet's face scrunches in disapproval of Graemes's haphazard journaling; the coblyn is secretly, proudly pleased to only use quality inks and charcoals in the birchbark, rather than 'any nearby thing' the way Graemes did in Curious Rituals. Thinking of this, the coblyn pats several pockets of extra inks and pen nibs.

Tonic continues, "But here, Graemes tells of meeting a dryad named Nightshade when they fought a gingerbread Curse together. The dryad got bound to the house, even though the battle exploded it! Nightshade lives deep in the epicenter of the Epicerie forest, and we should be able to learn something about Graemes there." Facet gives a slightly incredulous look, and Briny also looks doubtful, so Tonic adds, "The Epicerie isn't terribly far... I mean, I have at least *heard* of it, although I haven't actually *been*." Facet nods in acceptance, and Briny quickly calls the windrabbits over.

All three windrabbits have been swirling and tousling in rabbity games: Turbine is racing laps around Tonic's garden, Steam is playing Hide and Go Leaf, and Spindrift is bouncing in the creek, gathering rocks, shells, and cattails (then whipping them away as soon as the items are boring). At Briny's whistling call, the windrabbits breeze their way over.

Turbine nudges Facet, and hops impatiently, until the Coblyn offers a dusty treat for answering the call. Briny gives Spindrift some soap bubbles, and Tonic holds out a handful of dried cherry petals to Steam.

Coblyn, Gnome, and Sprite plan their route to find Nightshade in the Epicerie using Facet's maps and cartography skills. The coblyn is very excited to explain the newly-finished Stratigraphy Skirt, but after enthusing about layers of earth and geography and history, Facet is forced to admit that the horizontally-striped skirt doesn't do very well showing the surface of the world, and thus is not very useful for mapping their route to the Epicerie. Briny and Tonic nod and agree that the Stratigraphy Skirt is marvelous, even if they can't use it right now. Facet is clearly proud. Briny offers knowledge of the weather, and Tonic deciphers clues from Graemes's journal. From the regular, surface map that Facet shares (not as interesting as the stratigraphy layers under the earth, in Facet's opinion), the friends find that the Epicerie appears to be mostly wild forest and glade, with homes dotted sparsely throughout, and the very middle, the epicenter, seems to be a small village. According to the map, the roads to the village are old and rather unkempt.

"How will we get there?" Briny wonders, "I figured we would take the Quiltdown River or use a boat on the Diffuse Sea, but neither waterpath goes near the Epicerie. We *could* take a Stream of Consciousness, since they can go *any*where, but they are dreadfully difficult to get to a *specific* destination."

Facet nods thoughtfully. "Good observation! Rarebit Holes have similar difficulties; once you fall down one, you don't know where you'll end up, nor how long it'll take to get there. We could take some Hoppercarts, though! There is a HopStop not far from here." The coblyn pauses to adjust the goggles. "Although I doubt there are any HopStops to return the HopperCarts to, inside of the Epicerie; and the rough terrain might be too much for them. I think we should start with a Snakeline. We could take a Coachwhip or Blackracer most of the way to the Epicerie; they are both gleaming fast lines!"

Tonic nods agreement, "It's the quickest to get going, and we can walk from there. If we come across a better mode of travel on the way, we can always switch."

Emboldened by their purpose (find Graemes) and destination (very center of the spice-filled Epicerie forest) the trio feels ready to go! Ensuring provisions are tucked into their peach pack, bronze bag, and seafoam satchel, they begin their journey to the Epicerie; given their calculations, this trip shouldn't take more than a day or two at most. But just in case, each of them have packed a few extras, too.

The friends travel companionably aboard a Coachwhip Line, enjoying watching the rolling fields and playful woods of Meadows zip past their speedy Snakeline windows. "I've never traveled a Coachwhip Line before!" Facet remarks with a piqued interest; the coblyn scurries off to check out all parts of the gleaming and hissing mode of transport (and very much hoping to get to talk to the engineer). Briny tells Tonic with a bubbly laugh, "There's a Coral Line on the beach by my sandcastle. It's an older model Snake, so you hear the hissing and clacking much louder. Of course, many coblyns, knockers, and kobolds come to the shore just to ride the Line! They seem to love the older, louder, gear and steam-powered Snakelines."

Sooner than they think, the friends disembark at a station in a village not too far from the Epicerie. They have a late lunch of scone sandwiches, and after a brief debate about distance and cost, they forgo the HopperCarts and begin walking at a steady and relaxed pace, with songs, rests, conversations, and only occasional complaints. Mostly occasional. Adventures are difficult; adventures mean stretching yourself, trying new things, and going new places. Plus, it is still dreadfully hot for mid-autumn. The three friends are sweating within minutes. Adventures mean facing your comfort zone and going outside it, so there are *definitely* some complaints... But good companions make things better! And the windrabbits have enough adorable antics and breezy gusts to keep the group entertained through the first part of their journey on the road.

Chapter 5: Nightshade

After much landscape has passed, the day has worn on, and toes have definitely begun to tire, the three friends find they are walking along the path through a somewhat rocky, overgrown wood. A wooden sign is carved with the bold announcement "Epicerie" and has a painted border of spices. They are in the Epicerie Forest! The trees and undergrowth here remind Tonic of home, many of them give off tantalizing hints of savory and sweet. At first, the windrabbits rush around, brushing rushes and puffing up spicy scents, but eventually the aerial lagomorphs settle down. The forest gets deeper and darker as the friends continue on. As the day starts to blend into late afternoon, Tonic sniffs the air, nose tilting this way and that, head twisting to face different directions. Steam whistles a snore from within the travel teapot and the gnome pats the teapot and sniffs the air some more.

"What are you doing?" Briny askes the gnome with curiosity.

Tonic responds distractedly, "Smelling. There is a sort of, well, a new scent. I don't know what plant it belongs to... Have you ever stopped a task to follow a scent?" With eyes closed and nostrils twitching, the gnome continues, "I love finding a new scent. Right now, I want to know what that..." Tonic ponders, trying to find the right description... "that sort of deep, spicy, sweet scent is. It smells a bit burnt, in a good, cooled way; like a dark maple syrup."

Briny and Facet sniff too, but their noses aren't as honed for plant-scents as the gnome's tea-sniffing snout is. Tonic sniffs some more, and the friends set off in search of the scent's source while the gnome continues, "You both have a scent too you know. Briny, you smell fresh and breezy, kind of like lemongrass, ozone, salt, and rain..." Briny gleams with pride at the apt description, and smooths down some rainbows that have ruffled up in the cascading blue outfit.

"Facet, you tend to smell cool and earthy, like carrot or ginger, and moss and copper." Tonic finishes. Facet considers this, then makes a quick note with a bit of willow charcoal to sniff fresh carrot and ginger next time it's available. This leads to a list of possible scent blends, sketches of some herbs, and a design for a metal necklace that can hold scents and release them as the metals warm up. Finding it difficult to sketch or write while walking, the coblyn keeps the notes very brief.

The friends remain on the dirt path, not wanting to get lost in these unfamiliar woods; although they have seen several forest critters, they haven't met any other beings since entering the Epicerie. The forest around them is thick, and after such a lot of travel (and with the promise of twilight coming on) it has begun to feel ominous. Briny wishes for open air and more beings to talk to, and Facet is distracted by the million thoughts that there isn't time to write down. Tonic leads by a nose, following the sweet, spicy scent trail through the dense forest. There are occasional footpaths leading away to places unknown: maybe the village they saw on the map? Could they be getting close to the epicenter? Suddenly the trio comes to a clearing with a large, dilapidated house in the middle, which is made of a rich, tan bread, and Tonic declares it as the source of the delicious smell they have been following. There are intricate curls and swirls adorning the house around every door frame, window, and rail that remains; some of the decorations are carved, and some seem piped-on like frosting.

As Briny, Facet, and Tonic admire the decaying house's adornments in the softened light of almost-twilight, Facet wonders aloud, "Rickety rust! Would a knock on the door crash the whole thing down?" Then before they can act, an outraged **squeal** rings out of the surrounding forest!

From somewhere inside the gingerbread ruins, an enraged fury bursts upon the three friends, bluefire angry, and shrieking, "Nibble, nibble little mouse, who is nibbling at my house?!"

Briny and Facet try to ready defenses, grabbing gears and salting seaspray. Thoroughly terrified, Tonic grips the Mighty Teaspoon Hammer and only manages to whisper, "Um. No one. We aren't eating anything..." The three friends are ready to fight this violent being, or help each other flee, they aren't sure which.

While the gnome, sprite, and coblyn try to decide how to deal with the fury, a purple and green dryad runs up from behind the ruins, *tisk*ing and swiping at the snarling creature with a broom. "Oh no you don't! Pesky thing." Folding down luna-moth wings like a cloak, the dryad sags and smiles with relief when the fury dissipates like smoke. "My apologies," the dryad greets the friends in a smooth voice, while straightening a pale, star-shaped hat, and shaking dust off a much-buttoned purple and green vest and pants. "It's part of the curse's magic." The dryad gestures at the gingerbread remains with a rueful smile, "The fury isn't real *per se*, but it *can* hurt visitors. I've found a broom is best for clearing the triggered spell away."

Inspecting the indicated ruins, Facet notes that the dryad has spent effort reinforcing some of the walls, clearing away weeds, and setting up a bench and seats inside. The dryad has spent a lot of time to turn part of the ruins into a remarkable garden pergola!

"Whenever someone gets close, I am compelled to defend this ramshackle place because of the curse." the dryad continues, "I am trying to fix it up and dismantle the curse, but, clearly, I'm not done yet." The dryad turns to face the friends, gave a bow of greeting and says, "I go by Nightshade. How can I help you? Are you lost? The gingerbread scent does tend to lead people off their path."

"Actually, I think you ARE our path; We are on a quest." Briny states, recovering from the surprise with a head shake, which causes the sprite's hair to froth like stormy seas.

"A journey!" Tonic announces in agreement, patting a bit of frayed leaf embroidery on a petal pocket.

"An *adventure*." Facet supportively adds, making the tool belt pockets jangle.

"All that at once?" Nightshade asks. "Well, why don't you come in and tell me about it?" The dryad shows the coblyn, sprite, and gnome to a house off to one side, while chatting companionably. "This way! My house is a glorious little Aubergine, with a spacious Potato Root Cellar, and the best Sweet Tomato Shed! Look, I just renovated the belladonna-bloom roofing."

As the group approaches Nightshade's deep purple house, they can see behind the gingerbread ruins, to a fawn-colored mushroom cottage that has a leathery-looking roof. Briny stares at the bright red pools of liquid on the roof, and Facet assesses the matching red-paned windows with the ever-helpful gem-goggles.

"Do you like it?" Nightshade asks, noticing the rapt

attention. "I renovated that building myself. The Red Juicetooth is a great library! It has the comfiest fly agaric seats inside, and dozens of shelves! I live in the Aubergine, but friends often stay in the Juicetooth Library. See the mushrooms on the garden path?" Gnome, sprite, and coblyn turn to look at the unassuming fungi beside the trail that connects the purple house and tan library.

"Those are all bioluminescent!" Nightshade explains, "They light the path at night with their foxfire glow. Sometimes, if you sit very still, you can see the flickering vulpines who help light them up! They are tiny foxes, no bigger than beetles, and they love to play in the mushroom glow. Whoever built the gingerbread house *really* liked sweets and mushrooms; I'm pretty sure it was a distant cousin, from the Amanita side of my family, rather than the Solanaceae side. We are all related way back from the famous Tocsins, who split over some big fuss, and became Tocsins and Toxins." The dryad grins and adds proudly, "I have had to do a lot of research to properly fix the place up, and managed to learn more about my own family, as well as tons about sugar treats and fungi! Most of the glowing mushrooms are of the Mycenae group, but not all of them." While leading the group toward the Aubergine house, Nightshade starts pointing to different mushrooms and listing types. "I've found Panellus stipticus (those oyster-shaped ones, with a bright glow), honey mushrooms (by the tree; they are squat and sticky, with a yellow color), fairy helmets (these violet ones over here on the rotting log; they are tiny and grow in clusters), and jack-o-lanterns (the big orange ones here; only their gills glow)."

The group winds their way through the garden while Nightshade talks, finally arriving at the indigo door of the dryad's house. "Oh my geese! I've been so excited to share my work, I haven't let you talk! Please, come in and tell your story." The dryad opens the front door and invites

Tonic, Facet, and Briny into the deeply-purple house. Inside, Nightshade's house is clean and soft and white, with a mild, crisp scent. There is a wall with various-sized shelves carved into it, which Facet is drawn to; each shelf is filled with containers and unusual items. Several, or rather, *quite a few* shelves seem to be devoted to buttons: bags, boxes, vases, and piles of a glorious multitude of buttons in all shapes, sizes, and shades. There are also a vast array of boxes, most of which appear to be empty (although you never know what might be in an apparently empty container).

Seeing the coblyn's interest, "That's my Knicknackatory," Nightshade gestures, while also bringing some chairs over to the glossy, blue-green mushroom table (have you ever tried to gesture coherently while holding chairs? Nightshade doesn't recommend it). Amid a clatter of chairs and straightening them at the table, Nightshade continues, "Here, please sit, everybeing! I love buttons. I can't help but decorate my clothes with them." The friends, having noted the dryad's outfit, agree as Nightshade goes on, "And to store them in; boxes! There really is a delight about boxes; little drawers, bags, cubbyholes... they are always full of chaos and possibilities!"

Facet makes a few notes while Briny and Tonic listen with absorption, as Nightshade says, "A friend first introduced me to Knicknackatories as a place to keep and cherish memorabilia. Ha! Always considered it the best way to display memories and invite a little uncertainty. You seem to get the best stories that way, with a mix of history and the unknown; stories need change, difficulties, and growth. So, tell me about your story." Finishing the explanation, and inviting the friends to talk, Nightshade then waits patiently for the party to say what they want.

Realizing it's their turn to explain why they've come all this way, Tonic thinks of Graemes's journal, the Wanderlust, and the recent Conclusions, and isn't sure what to say.

Would the dryad be willing or able to help them? An adventure to find a friend who says they go to Mythwold; honestly, no being could take them seriously! Tonic is frozen with indecision, and absent-mindedly taps the Mighty Teaspoon Hammer.

Briny's feet shuffle under the table (making the sprite's outfit wave and ripple), waiting for Tonic, and Facet gives a "you're in the lead" gesture. Tonic feels bolder knowing that the sprite and coblyn both give their support. Taking the lead, the gnome inhales deeply and speaks up. "Nightshade, we want to find where Graemes went."

The dryad is quiet with surprise for a moment, then replies with kindness, "Oh, Graemes! One of the best, most adventurous friends I've ever met. And more prone to randomly disappear than anyone I ever met, too!" The dryad gives a loving laugh. "Yes, Graemes has traveled a lot, and every time we meet up again, it's just as comfortable and lovely as before. It's so good to have a friend who can come and go and always be just as good a friend as ever." The three friends nod agreement as Nightshade pauses. Then the dryad continues, suggesting, "Truthfully, Graemes is probably traveling the World's Between. Graemes is always going there and returning to tell me stories of the Mythwold." Briny, Facet, and Tonic look a combination of dubious and shocked; does this dryad expect them to believe the World of Myth is *really* real?

Noting the guests' somewhat horrified expressions, Nightshade assures them, "It's okay! The World of Myth is real, but not as terrible as the stories make it seem. Graemes is going there and back all the time. Mythwold is apparently full of broken cities of tar and poison and stone, but of wonderful things too; the Sighing Ants create powerful magic of lightning and metal. And I believe Graemes says they call Fierlund 'fairy land,' ... a somewhat silly name, I think."

Briny cuts in, "Do you know which way the wind blows

to the World's Between?" and Tonic adds, "We've just got to find Graemes!" The gnome looks uncertain and continues, holding up *Curious Rituals of Uncommon Folk*, "I've looked through this book, but a lot of it is hard to read. There are smudges and stains, and I think some pages are missing. Most of the ones that are left are crinkled. From what I can tell, Graemes never actually wrote down the exact HOW to travel the Worlds' Between."

Nightshade answers, "The World's Between isn't always easy to get to; Graemes swore the surest way was for a being to find a forgotten place, or a lost thing. Travel will change you, and traveling the World's Between will change you Wildlings muchly."

"How do we find forgotten places? I mean... if they are forgotten, then how do we find maps to them? Can anyone direct us? Do we just wander around hopefully?" Facet asks querulously.

"I don't know. All the forgotten places I have found (which only total 2) I stumbled upon." Nightshade points to a map on the wall. "You can ask at the Story Orchard, though. Even if a thing is largely forgotten, the Librarians probably have a record of it. Let me draw you a map and you can start fresh in the morning." Turning around, the dryad sees Facet in good lighting and Nightshade's mouth drops open, then the dryad blurts out, "is that a Stratigraphy Skirt?! Can you shake it out? I have never seen one fully realized before! I will mark the Orchard on there too, if you like. Does it really work? The Librarians would be so intrigued!"

Facet obligingly gives the skirt a sharp shake, which causes terrain to pop up, or down, all over it. Nightshade, Briny, and Tonic all marvel at the amazing skirt which has formed into different layers of dirt below and different heights of topography on top. Once Nightshade has grabbed the correct map, unbuttoned it, and finished marking the Orchard on the skirt, Facet gives another quick shake, and the Stratigraphy Skirt is back to its usual flat, striped self.

Nightshade looks at how late it is and offers the trio dinner, "If you can help me dig up some sweet potatoes." Tonic is pleased to do that task, using the Mighty Teaspoon Hammer to scoop potatoes out of the ground. Once that is finished, Nightshade fixes everybeing a dinner of buttery-baked sweet potatoes and tomato soup; Briny is delighted to assist, making a seaweed salad, and creating a pie for dessert with some of Nightshade's sweet potatoes and the dried fruits and nuts Tonic packed. Facet, meanwhile, sketches some ideas from the dryad's map, then helps fill mushroom bowls and gingerbread plates with the mouth-watering meal. When the food is all prepared, Nightshade invites everyone out to the pergola to eat dinner in the sweet night air. The dryad cautions the trio not to touch the remains of the gingerbread house, since there is still a lot of sticky curse-residue.

Once settled in the pergola, Facet offers Nightshade some silver Glamour coins for the room and board. "We can't possibly eat your food, dirty your dishes, and use your beds without repaying you somehow!" Face insists. Nightshade politely declines, "Just make sure you let me know how Graemes is doing, and send that dusty old traveler to visit me! That trade would be good repayment" Tonic promises they will tell Graemes to go visit. The group enjoys the meal, feeding nibbles to the windrabbits, and watching as the bioluminescent mushrooms start to glow along the path. Peering carefully with Nightshade's direction, they get to see the nearly-invisible fiery foxes flying gleefully down the path, and playing in the mushrooms' glows.

After the food is finished and the foxes have fled, Facet starts to take out the Night Tent, but Nightshade insists they all sleep in the Juicetooth Library. The Juicetooth is clean and dry and filled with comfy cushions, so the tired trio have no problem falling asleep.

Chapter 6: Unicorn Guide

When the sky is light, Briny, Facet, and Tonic break their fasts with Nightshade; everyone enjoys leftovers from the night before. Then the friends set out for the Story Orchard with marked maps in hand. Having put down roots while trying to fix the gingerbread curse, Nightshade is unable to lead the friends to the Orchard; the dryad instead introduces the friends to a pleasant unicorn guide. Mushroom is no bigger than Facet's hand, with a creamy white coat and bright red mane, tail, and hooves.

"Just follow Mushroom! The little unicorn is always running errands to and from the Orchard and has agreed to guide you for a small fee. Do you have some copper beans you can spare? Mushroom is small and doesn't need much coin." Seeing the trio nod in agreement, Nightshade waves them on and calls from the gingerbread ruins, "Well met, and meet again!" Dryads, as you may know, are attached to their plants, and cannot travel beyond them without great sacrifice. Nightshade waves again to the group, wishing them well until they are out of sight.

Facet digs out a few copper Bean coins and puts them in Mushroom's saddlebag saying, "We would appreciate you leading us to the Ideas Orchard." The small, round unicorn nods and struts down the path jauntily. Mushroom likes to whinny songs while trotting, and although they don't speak unicorn, each friend feels the joy in the little tunes. All of a sudden, Mushroom steps off the well-worn path, and follows a twisting trail of slippery roots and rotting fungi. This overgrown path appears rarely frequented, and the once wide, welcoming wood quickly yields to a dark and dense forest.

The friends feel that leaving a well-traveled path is always an uncertain thing; it can be dangerous to forge a new path, but there may be great rewards, too. Mushroom seems confident, and the trio don't know any other way to the Story Orchard, so they follow along, anxiously paying attention to their surroundings. Tonic warns them not to step on any plants, as they might be rare, or could have thorns that scratch, or oils that itch. "Every plant is an important part of the environment," the gnome reminds them.

The group travels on, following the merry tapping of Mushroom's tiny hooves, and mindful of the foliage. The path forged by the unicorn is long and arduous. It twists, and drips, and not much light gets through, especially as the mist builds up. The air is drenched in sweaty vapors, and unseen insects buzz and click. More insects drift in sudden clouds that the friends walk through, and even (bleh!) breathe in. Tiny, unseeable bugs crawl on the trio and bite them, leaving tiny, itchy welts. In the gloom of the path, coblyn, sprite, and gnome find themselves chatting less, curling in on their own discomforts, feeling snappish at Mushroom's silly songs, and growing distant from each other. The journey is uncomfortable and tiring; they go up hills and down, climb over massive roots, stumble on slippery rocks, and feel thirsty and grimy. Briny's hair turns dark and still, like eerie ponds, and the sprite's fluttery outfit is sodden and tangled. In some places the fog is so thick that they all feel as if they are constantly walking into a white wall; and sometimes they *do* walk right into obstacles, when the path turns unexpectedly, or the fog is particularly opaque. Facet's vine hair-tie frays, and opal strands of hair get in the coblyn's eyes. The friends talk even less, and grumble internally about the sticky temperature, loud bugs, itchy plants, and bruised limbs. Slowly Mushroom's tapping fades into the fog, and each friend becomes slower and more focused on their own worries:

"No one listens to me... Can I make a difference? ...It doesn't really matter... Keeping so much junk... Gnomes aren't good leaders anyway... Feeling so trapped... Sprites can't understand my troubles... just wanted to see new places!... Coblyns don't do real work... Is my job actually important?... I'd like to help, but I'm scared... What if I mess up?... Always jumping into new things... Too focused on one idea..." and on and on their doubts and prejudices grow.

Soon, the cheerful unicorn is no longer leading them. The path is no longer marked. The thick fog obscures almost everything.

All three friends feel querulous and uncommunicative. They mope and grouse, and cannot focus on solving their dilemma. The trio is so self-absorbed and focused on difficulties, they hardly remember that they are trying to get to the Story Orchard.

A disgruntled forever slowly elapses.

Settling into a sullen stupor, the gnome, sprite, and coblyn can't tell how much time is passing; it seems to stretch on interminably, each minute growing more irritable than the last. The group's thoughts are all smooshed into one gloomy, dreary, oppressive mood.

"How do we get out of here?" Briny sulks. "And where's the clippy mini-corn?" Spindrift spins in stagnant circles, and the sprite's complexion looks like deep and dangerous waters. The water sprite coaxes a rain cloud down to make a cold, dank puddle for wallowing in. Briny and Spindrift sink down in the murky water.

Facet fusses with an uneaten raincake, then uses it to act as a lens and starts a small, smokey fire-smudge in a small patch of moist lichens. After putting on the spectacular goggles, the coblyn vengefully tears up the broken vine hair tie, and rips pieces out of the Birchbark Journal and feeds the forlorn fragments to the damp fire.

In a snit, Tonic collects twigs to start a better fire and make tea. "Nothing is going right. We may as well stay *here* forever," the gnome gripes. With each strike of flint and steel, Tonic lists another complaint, "The plants are wrong," *snikt* "the weather is wrong," *click* "the ground is wrong." *fwish* "We are lost" *skrit* "and no one is helping!" *fwoosh!* The gnome angrily makes tea, grumpily spilling leaves and sloshing the brew, which only increases Tonic's bitter mood. "Ugh! This is making me waste good ingredients! Stupid quest. Stupid adventure." Tonic sips the imperfect tea vengefully, which is mildly soothing, but provides no good answers.

Facet picks up a burned twig and grumpily sketches what an Idea Orchard might look like. The sketch is very stabby, and has a dark and moody tone.

Watching the coblyn thrash at the page, Tonic quickly stands up "Facet, that is a great idea! ...Briny! We are looking for an orchard. It will be more open and spacious than this dratted forest. Can you figure out the weather? Which way feels open like 'orchard'?"

Briny's expression clearly says "this is hopeless" but the sprite checks the wind, the clouds, the sun, and asks

Spindrift to run above the trees for a better weather view.

Determined to be useful, Tonic tries to assess their assets. "Facet, didn't Nightshade mark the Story Orchard on your Stratigraphy Skirt? Let's have a look. How does this work?"

Facet's eyes open wide as the coblyn wakes up from depressing self-doubt. "Oh, yes!" Facet adjusts the goggles like a headband to hold the gemstone hair in check, "The skirt shows the layers of geological history under our feet. It changes as the layers of soil beneath us change." Twisting to look around the skirt, Facet points to the inked book and tree Nightshade drewf, and announces "We are almost there! Look, there is barely any stratigraphy between us and the orchard."

"Judging from the Weather Tendencies, I say we just need to go through the darkest patch of woods over there." Briny explains, in a grudgingly hopeful tone.

"Great!" Tonic cheers; although the gnome doesn't feel completely joyful yet, the appreciation is genuine and the gnome wants to encourage everybeing. "Thank you both for your hard work. Facet, your pictures of the path and Orchard really helped jog me out of my funk. Briny, you responded quickly and efficiently. I don't think we ever would have gotten out without working together!"

Briny keeps a weather-eye out and leads the way through the dreary, dense clumps of forest while Facet makes course corrections using the Stratigraphy Skirt.

Chapter 7: Story Orchard

As they emerge from the dripping, shadowed forest tangle, a Librarian with ink-embellished skin and short, straight, parchment-white hair is tending some trees. The Librarian greets them, "Oh my works uncited, we weren't expecting visitors today! Hello there; I go by Vellum. I am one of the Librarians here in the Story Orchard. How can we assist you?" Mushroom stands by the librarian's feet, chirruping happily, then skip-trots away once Facet, Briny, and Tonic are all in view. The orchard has bright, hot, post-midday light in the open areas, and pleasant pools of shade beneath the trees.

"What was that awful swamp-forest about?! It must have taken hours to travel through! Why did Mushroom leave us? I think we were nearly lost forever!" Briny bursts out, and the sprite's hair puffs like rolling storm clouds.

Vellum tends to some scrollwork leaves on a tree, checking for any signs of ill-health in the plant and distractedly responds, "Ah, yes. You must have been following the unicorn; Mushroom has trotted off to the stables for a snack. The Preconceived Woods are perilous, but just about the only way here. Many get lost in their own thoughts, trapped in their old ideas, and never make it out of those woods. You are lucky you had such a helpful unicorn to lead you so far! I believe your self-absorption caused you to lose sight of your guide. Still, you must have a good friendship to have stayed focused nearly the whole way here. The Preconceived Woods around the Orchard reminds us that we must work through our own fears and biases before we are ready to learn new ideas. I find it best to work together, stand up for each other, and say NO to bad thinking while there. Be willing to admit when you are wrong and listen to what others tell you; it helps immensely. And, of course, if you have a guide, ensure you follow it." Vellum finishes with a wry smile. The Librarian turns toward the biggest trees, carved and sculpted into a magnificently towering structure, "Grotto! Please have the incunabula wait a moment, and bring some new ideas for our guests." From a treetop window, a young figure with many braids is seen to scurry; Grotto arrives shortly with a stack of books, shakes out a cloth one-handed, lays it onto a stump with a flourish, places the stack of books down on top, then hurries off again.

"We need to learn about forgotten places." Facet volunteers. "We are helping Tonic on a Wanderlust, and need to travel...what was it?"

"The World's Between. Nightshade recommended we ask here." Tonic finishes.

"Ah," Vellum replies. "Take a journal to chew on and walk with me through the Story Orchard while I work on a list for you."

Inspecting the stack of books closer, Facet points out the plate underneath them. Briny cautiously picks up a journal and peers at it. Tonic nervously rubs a patch of arm-moss, then swiftly chooses a journal and takes a bite. "These are so good!" the gnome announces with delight, while spraying some crumbs. Briny and Facet each quickly choose a journal to snack on, remarking on the sweet-savory flavor, and flaky, pastry-like crust.

Vellum leads the group, softly sharing the life and habits of the Orchard. The Librarian's love of the Story Orchard, though quiet, is unmistakable. Vellum's voice becomes suffused with joy when talking about the Orchard.

Gesturing at the wide variety of trees in the orchard, all spaced neatly and evenly for maximum growth and nutrition, Vellum says, "All around us are the Book Trees. Gather close! See the small word buds? They are smooth and easy to use. Touch them; aren't they comfy? These word buds are perfect for beginner Librarians. We start our training as soon as we can stand up, and word buds are often low on the tree, within easy reach for young hands and minds. If encouraged to flourish, the word buds will bloom into fantastic, and often loquacious, elegance. Look at those stunning narrative blossoms!" Vellum points to some bright, intricate flowers high up in some of the trees.

Facet pats some of the small word buds, thinking about all of the things they could become. "What a fascinating way to create!" the coblyn enthuses. "It is much like crafting and inventing. These are the building blocks and gears needed to realize something more elaborate!" Vellum smiles and encourages Facet to keep a word bud, which the coblyn gratefully presses into the birchbark journal.

Walking in the soothing shade of many different trees, Vellum points out more parts of the orchard, "Here are some curious leaflets, they encourage the tree-tender to keep asking and searching. A curious leaflet can go a long way towards helping you complete research; they often have surprising, interesting facts, and they lead us to explore more. These are very useful for those needing to hold or gain interest."

Briny lets Spindrift play in the curious leaflets, and the windrabbit races through the tree, wildly rattling leaflets and notions. Turbine and Steam soon wake and poke their noses out of Facet's bronze bag and Tonic's travel teacup. The sociable Zephyrs join the Gale, playing a game of tag all through the tree.

"That's enough, you three. Don't shake the young leaflets off!" Briny admonishes with a laugh. The windrabbits flow out of the trees, whirling and bouncing between the group's ankles instead.

Vellum continues to show more of the orchard, explaining differences in leaf shape, trunk patterns, growth habits, and nutritional needs of the trees. After some time, the group comes to a new section of Orchard. The Librarian grins widely and announces, "Over here are words ripe for picking."

Each guest gets to try a word. Facet has "plethora" Briny chooses "indubitably" and Tonic picks "prodigious." Vellum encourages, "Try out your new words! Roll the words around in your mouth; taste the texture. Each word is unique and lends a different flavor to what you say. Consider 'worried' and 'hysterical.' The two words mean nearly the same thing, but in very different flavors!" Sharing their fantastic new words and experimenting with how to use them, the friends agree that the Story Orchard is magnificent.

Vellum skips along a short way, to even larger trees, spaced further apart. "Ripe books are stored in the shelf-like hollows of Book Trees. These are where we store the majority of our finished works. Scrolls live in smaller trees, tomes in sturdier ones. Our filing system is largely bark. You can tell a Book Tree's contents by the words grown into the bark. This one here is traditional poetry on scrolls; see the words formed repeatedly in the bark?"

Happy to share knowledge and guide a tour, the Librarian is full of joy showing the group around. "Over here we have a small quarry for refining glimmering nuggets of an idea.

These little gems form from the crystalized resin when a tree is wounded. Excess letters and grammar can be used here to scrub and grind crystalized ideas, sloughing off biases and hypocrisies to refine the ideas." Facet lingers to admire the beautiful, polished resins.

An area rich with dark earth and dotted with mounds comes next. Tonic is excited to see such healthy compost piles, knowing how important decomposition is for plants to gain nutrients. Vellum explains, "Sometimes ideas become outdated, and the books get squishy and overripe. These books must be unshelved and planted so new ideas can grow out of the old. These books will rot and decompose, creating fertile ground for the seeds of new ideas."

The three friends are agog with wonder at the Story Orchard, and have almost forgotten the reason that they had come there when Vellum says, "To your purpose; those with a strong connection to the World's Between, we call them Wildlings. Have you ever felt a longing for a place you've never been? Have you been truculent, recalcitrant, or stubborn? Looked up the meaning of a word just because you liked how it felt on your tongue? Have you felt a Wanderlust so strong, you just had to go, but you didn't know where? Have you felt different than those around you? These are all aspects of being a Wildling, and of the ability to travel the World's Between."

Tonic gasps to hear such experiences described so exactly.

Vellum reads from a book titled "Curious Rituals of Uncommon Folk" and says "I have here a copy of a Wildling's first-hand account. It says here the author, Graemes, was the first to call those from other realities "Wildlings" and also referred to them as 'someone from over the horizon.' Although this author is the first written mention of the word, there is some evidence that the word somehow wound it's way here from Mythwold." Holding the place with a finger, Vellum continues, "Although it was once commonly accepted to use 'Wildling' for those who cross the World's Between, over time fewer beings traveled the World's Between, and the word fell out of use and was largely forgotten. Just like the knowledge that Mythwold is real."

The Librarian closes the book, saying, "The Wildlings who Travel the World's Between live among us. They are real. We don't often see them, because the roads to travel are... sort of next to us, invisible, and insubstantial. But Wildlings *can* get to them, although nearly everyone has forgotten how. There used to be many Wildlings, many who knew how to travel the World's Between."

Briny, Facet, and Tonic stand still, stunned.

Finally Tonic asks with a splutter, "How do you have that book?"

Vellum replies with a warm smile, "Oh, every book ever written grows a copy here in the Orchard! Many books do not get past a few scattered words or phrases; that is where a lot of our word buds and leaflets come from. But if a book is well formed enough, it grows into a full copy of the work and gets shelved here."

While the friends marvel at this information, Grotto walks up with a single scroll, orchard-light dappling on freckles, muscular arms, and bouncing mahogany hair braids. Vellum speaks to the friends as Grotto hands them the scroll; "Here is a list of forgotten places within travel from here: The Tree Beyond the Garden, The Hole in the Bottom of the Sea, The Witch of the Westmoreland, Walking Grass on the Heath, the Bog of the Dead Moon, and the Scent from Childhood. There aren't many options anywhere nearby, I'm afraid. You will need to seek out the forgotten places, because realities grow thin and touch there; our persistent myths come from places where realities leak. Find a forgotten place that makes your blood sing and your senses glow. There will be a Lintel of the World's Between close by. You have your list. Where will you choose to go?"

Chapter 8: Hoppercarts

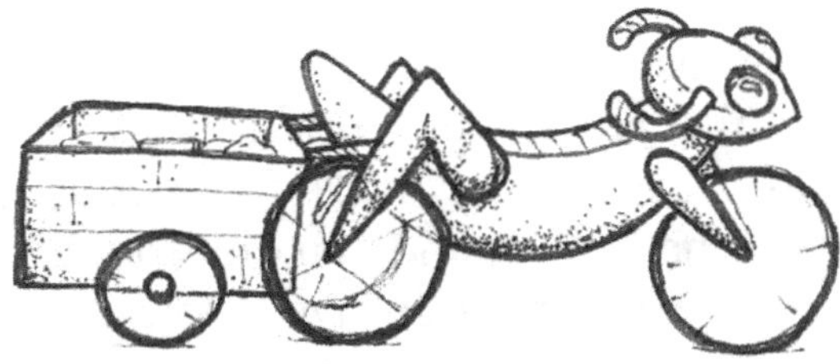

Once inside the cool, still shade of a Quercus Alba tree, the group sits at a table and goes over their options, while eating a midday snack. The Librarians provide a plethora of fresh fruits and nuts, and Tonic makes an energizing batch of tea. Briny checks on the windrabbits, ensuring they are all groomed, fed, and cared for. Facet uncaps ink and gets a fresh nib to write notes in the birchbark journal as Vellum offers knowledge and advice.

The Librarian's voice is clear, listing off thoughts and suggestions. Facet writes quickly, adding to a list of new words, sketches, and meanings:

Marginalia – References the beautiful in the borders. In a work of writing, marginalia are doodles and illustrations, sometimes even notations, in the borders and margins around the main text. Not the main story, but the most interesting enhancements. Marginalia is also the name for the things that guard the Lintels to the World's Between.

Lintel - the exact spot or feeling that allows a Wildling to travel the World's Between. These are often in forgotten places, or found on a Wanderlust. Guarded by Marginalia.

World's Between - How we travel to other realities, alongside our own. Tonic tried to explain this idea with a teapot universe and tealeaf realities. The World of Myth is where we end up (the World of Myth is where all our mythology really lives, stuff like sabertooth oxen and stone speaking and writing twigs that bleed color).

Mythwold, or the World of Myth - the place where our mythic tales come from. All the fantasy dreamed of is basically something real in the World of Myth; back when more Wildlings traveled the World's Between they brought explanations of what they found and did from the World of Myth, and those turned into our mythic tales.

Fairyland - the word for our own Fierlund. It seems to be a mix of 'fair' and 'fear;' beings from Mythwold believed Wildlings to be some sort of spirits they call 'fairies.'

Glazed - one who cannot travel the World's Between.

Wildling - one who can travel the World's Between, to the World of Myth. Tend to long for other places and ideas. Often feel like they don't quite fit in. A word Graemes started? Now used for our traveling handcart merchants and storytellers.

Vellum wraps up the discussion, saying, "Wherever you go, Wildlings, travel boldly and joyfully! You are on a Wanderlust, and you are exploring new things; enjoy what you learn and change. Remember that you may end up in places you don't like; when that happens, realize that while you can't alter decisions you already made, you CAN always make new ones from where you are. And relish time with friends." Vellum then waits quietly for the trio to decide where they will go.

After looking at maps and taking into account the

warnings about the Marginalia being guardians, the friends decide to set out for the Tree Beyond the Garden. "The tree seems easiest to reach from here" Facet decides. Briny and Tonic agree. "How much is it to buy the map?" Facet asks.

Vellum replies, "You can borrow it for a trade we hold, or you can buy it for a Pot." Facet rummages through pockets, and Turbine helps. It is the windrabbit who wins the search, snuffling a gold-colored coin with a pot and rainbow etched on it out of Facet's pocket. The coblyn pays for the map, and gives Turbine a grit treat for a pocket well-searched. Briny adds some coppery Beans for the midday snacks the Librarians provided.

Thanking them, Vellum takes the coins and marks the way on the map for the trio and explains the path they should start on. "The map should serve you well, take care of it. I hope you find what you are looking for; please stop by and tell us your tales when you are done. In fact, here," Vellum hands the trio a small sheaf of colored papers, "write to us, should the fancy strike you. Well met, and meet again!" A few extra coins also earn the friends some Story Certificates to make their way out of the Orchard easier than the way in was.

Tonic, Facet, and Briny wave to the Librarians as they set out, with windrabbits flitting to and fro. The way out of the Story Orchard *is* easier than the way in; The three friends each carry a note from Vellum, penned in Story Ink and stamped with their windrabbit's paw prints, easing their travel through the Preconceived Woods.

Once out in the open again, they quickly find a road, and see several beings returning some Hoppercarts to a HopStop. The friends hurry up, and examine the vehicles available: Hoppercarts are common in Fierlund, and easily accessed (anybeing can rent one just by putting a silver Glamour in the attached box, which releases the Hoppercart. Then when you return it to any Hop Stop, you get 2 copper Beans back and the Hoppercart locks at the new stop.) They look something like a combination of a tricycle and a grasshopper, and they usually have a good sized basket for carrying many items. The ones at this Hop Stop are brightly colored and in good repair: Facet grabs a glossy green and bronze one with clacking gears, Briny decides on a teal one with yellow trim, and Tonic chooses a smooth olive and spring green one. The road is long, but not arduous. There are open fields, gentle hills, and pleasant trees along the path. The travel while pedaling the Hoppercarts is easy, and the friends make good time the first day.

That evening, Facet pulls a bundle out of the bronze bag with the exaltation, "We get to try my Night Tent!" The coblyn sets up the tent, with gears clicking into place, and canvas stretched taut. The beautiful tent is the glorious riot of a setting sky, dappled with shining stars that gently glow. The completed structure is approximately a cylinder, but with a cone roof. The tent easily fits the three friends inside and is sparsely furnished with 2 small but sturdy bunk beds, and a special netted shelf near the ceiling for holding food and things off the ground. The bunk beds are dark wood, with tan comforters, and red, yellow, and green sheets; they remind the friends of sandwiches, and they all decide it's time for dinner.

As Briny redirects some blustery wind traffic outside ("Don't you pull at that tent! On your way now; off through the forest!"), Facet fixes salad and scones for supper. The coblyn is excited to use the metal travel cooking set tinkered just for this journey. Tonic makes tea in the travel teapot, gently pouring out Steam first, and muses out loud, "I could have shown Vellum my journal Graemes wrote! I wonder what the Librarians think of the written works versus the grown copies? Would the two versions look exactly the same? Would there be differences, like ink splotches and sketches? Is Facet's notebook growing somewhere there?"

Facet clatters the metal dishes in surprise, and with a flutter of hands, nearly leaves the dishes dangling in the air, to rush off and write "Librarians, can you read this? Does the previous page have a drop of something green on it?" Picking up a small flower spilled from the salad the coblyn continues, "Does your copy have a flower pressed just here?" Then inking-in an arrow, Facet quickly adds, "What type is it?"

When the trio is sitting together and ready to eat, Briny asks brightly, "What happens to all the Sudden Ideas, Facet? You find so many, but hardly have more than 2 or 3 running around."

Facet nods, and answers with an eagerness to share knowledge, "Sudden Ideas take a lot of care. Somebeings can tend to many of them at once; I'm only good with two or three. Some Sudden Ideas are released when a creator realizes they can't care for it. Others go dormant and ultimately slip away if they aren't given enough attention; they will run around until anotherbeing finds them. The few I'm attending to, I let live in my birchbark journal. I make sure I tend and groom them, so they grow stronger and more useful."

"Oh, wow!" Briny exclaims. "So, any new Sudden Ideas you find, you have to decide to let an old idea go, or let the new one go?"

"Well, if I find a really good one, I hold onto it for a bit. I can keep a few extra if I let some be dormant a while." Facet answers "But yes, basically I have to choose which two or three to keep, and which to release. I know whichever ones I release will be happy until picked up by somebeing else. Sometimes I trade them to other coblyns." The friends watch the windrabbits play as they finish their meal and think over their day.

The three friends soon finish eating and cleaning up; Tonic puts away the leaf-shaped cups, Briny packs the wave-frothed bowls, and Facet organizes the metal pans. As they are settling down for sleep, Tonic finds a legible spot in Graemes's journal and reads aloud, "Then bronze and sunset Keph'thysa'at gave me a dragon's hug and said, 'Oh my changeling child: my child of the wyrd and wild, child of rough and unreasonable. Your power lies in your curiosity and your ferocity. Use your powers for good - explore, help, create, stand up for those in need, bring kindness and laughter and wonder to the world...'"

Thinking on this, the gnome decides to read their tea leaves before they all go to sleep. After a quick brew-up, Tonic pauses to decipher the leaf patterns in Facet's cup, "There is a great change coming, and we must all be ready to stand together. We mustn't doubt ourselves or give up. We need to accept each other's strengths and differences...Hmm; the leaves are not as precise as usual. They generally like to tell me things like 'There is a cake waiting for you. It tastes sweet.' or 'You need to do laundry today.' Well, maybe the next cup will be clearer."

Taking Briny's cup before the sprite can wash it out, Tonic says, "Briny, your powerful emotions will be needed soon. I think you will face a grave enemy..." the gnome hesitates, and turns the cup around, "Or you will need to recite a hidden poem. It's odd; normally these two leaf patterns aren't interchangeable, but I just can't tell which this is meant to be." The gnome of tea looks at the last cup and says, "Ah! To break our fast we will find some delicious nasturtiums, borage, rose, and violets! That's more like my usual leaf-readings. And the leaves remind me to use the mushroom powder from Nightshade as a broth." Pleased with the solid advice, Tonic lays all the soggy leaves out on a rock for the windrabbits to nibble through the night.

The tent is quiet and cool, despite the sticky heat outside. As the friends inside go to sleep, the canvas stars twinkle soothing patterns. From outside, the tent blends into the muggy night, and is nearly impossible to see.

In the morning, Facet folds up the tent, trying to persuade the canvas and the jeweled-gears to compress back into the envelope-sized star shape it began in. The whole thing jangles and twists, leaping out of Facet's hands, and being a nuisance. The Night Tent is difficult until Tonic sits down nearby, polishing the Mighty Teaspoon Hammer, and asking if any assistance is needed. The Night Tent jolts and shambles less in the coblyn's hands with the Mighty Teaspoon Hammer glinting in the morning light.

Facet laughs, "I guess sometimes even tents can decide to be less troublesome, with the threat of your freshly polished Teaspoon hovering nearby! The tent only works at night; it hides us and protects us." Facet explains "But during the day, the Night Tent is noisy and jittery. If I set it up too early it always just comes out as a squashed sandwich. The blasted thing is impossible to fold back up correctly once the sky is light, too. If I had remembered to pack it earlier, it would have twirled up like a musical chime, spinning starlight into pre-dawn symphonies. That's why it's a Night Tent. It only works properly at night. Well, now it's a half-wrecked cube; that will have to do for today." Facet shrugs acceptance and ties the Night Tent on top of the bronze bag.

The friends don't break their fast right away, but wait and gather the tea-leaf-predicted edible flowers along their route. They rest at the top of a large hill to make the mushroom broth and eat sugared petals; rose, borage, nasturtium, and calendula make a brightly colored sweet treat. The land spreads out below them, and the sky is wide open above. The plants lie low and soft on the ground. In the distance, a mountain range rises up, majestically soaring, slopes green with forests, and grand, snowy, clouded peaks at the top. From the heat of the oppressive autumn, the friends are excited to head toward the mountain's snowy slopes. The windrabbits frisk toward the freshening breeze of the mountain, and the ocean beyond.

By midday, Briny, Facet, and Tonic have nearly reached the mountain proper. They return their Hoppercarts to a Hop Stop on the road, and finish trekking to the base of the mountain. Briny points out a tasty snack, "Look, Tonic! Some young tomatoes!" The sprite indicates a cluster of plants with small, green, cherry-sized fruits and oak-ish leaves growing near their path.

"Oh, no!" Tonic warns, "See the thorns on the stems, and the wide lobes of the leaves? That is horse nettle! A poisonous member of the Solanaceae plants. We will have to look for another snack."

The mountain looks grey and rocky up close, with foreboding, jagged cliffs and icy, whipping winds further up the pinnacle. At the base of the mountain is a large, clean tunnel with a gate locked across it and a sign posted. The Mountain Gate sign says "Short Tunnel closed until Seasons return." There are two smaller signs pointing to trails on the right and left. Both trails wind up the mountain. The sign to the left says "Restore the Seasons" and the sign to the right says "Never Return."

"Well that's sinister." Briny says with crossed arms, looking at the sign to the right.

"I don't like the idea of Never Return." Facet agrees, hands tapping nervously.

"Easy enough," with a quick hair-pat Tonic decides, "let's find out what Restore the Seasons is about. Maybe whatever is down that path will allow us to use the Short Tunnel on our way back."

In agreement, the trio of friends start up the perilous-looking path to the left. Spindrift, Turbine, and Steam race joyfully along the path, frisking in the brisk gusts coming down from the summit, and playing a game of Motes and Eddies. Coblyn, sprite, and gnome hike up the steep incline, bracing against the slippery path and the pushing mountain breezes. The temperature gets colder as they climb.

Chapter 9: Season Knights

After a few hours' climb, huffing and puffing, the friends finally reach a leveled area. The air is colder here, distinctly crisp and chilly. Taking out a gear-patterned brocade duster, Facet is glad they thought to pack jackets. This part of the mountain is a riot of color, the trees all decked out in their best and brightest hues. The trail is covered with crunchy leaves, and nuts are everywhere, ready for picking. The windrabbits race through the fallen foliage, stirring them up into whorls and swirls of rattling color. Apples, walnuts, figs, gourds, and persimmons all peek through the underbrush just off the path, and hints of prickling frost whisper just beyond the senses. There is the distant lure of cider and campfire.

"This is the *perfection* of Autumn," Facet says dreamily, "all those bits of Autumn most loved, squished together into one perfect-painting moment." Scooping up some ochre mud Facet continues, "I bet there is a harvest festival just up ahead. We should get some apple crisps!" The coblyn starts sketching leaves and gourds using different shades of dirt from the ground.

Tonic brews them each a mug of cinnamon-y tea and uses the Mighty Teaspoon Hammer to stir the air above the cups to cool them. The gnome happily breathes in the faint, drifting smell of campfire, and does a happy twirl. "It's been so hot lately, somehow both humid AND parched... I had forgotten how BLISSFUL Autumn is!"

Briny sips the warming drink, and curls up with Spindrift on a seat-height rock. The sprite is dreamily knitting the clouds into a rainy grey, when suddenly Briny grunts grumpily, "What is *that* up there?"

Ahead of the three friends, further down the path, an intricately-worked bronze statue stands, blocking the way forward. The trio leaves their Autumnal enjoyments to examine the obstacle; there is no way around it, as the statue abuts the cliff going up on its right shoulder, the sheer drop down on its left side, and nasty thorns filling in any possible cracks and discouraging ideas of climbing. The statue's armor is patterned to look like sheaves of wheat, with cornucopia of ripe fruits and vegetables meeting in the middle of the breastplate. A full quiver is slung across the knight's back, and a sturdy hunting bow is held in one hand. On the other side rests a shield, depicting a wounded deer, and a field of stars. The bronze knight stands in mud-caked boots on a rocky bronze path strewn with curling bronze leaves and oakcorns. The whole thing looms ominously tall. At close inspection, Facet notices a cloud and lightning pattern on the helm and gauntlets. The plaque beneath the statue says "Blood Knight."

"Well, what now?" Tonic wonders aloud. "We can't really stay in Autumn forever, and it looks like there might be a task to complete before we can go forward. My Mighty

Teaspoon Hammer can act as a shield against the thorns off the path, but it doesn't really help us get past the sheer drop or the sheer incline beside this towering, looming statue."

Facet muses, "The statue stands like a sentry or guard, blocking the path. Maybe we need to fulfill a task for the Blood Knight so that we can pass."

Briny lashes out "Who is giving their blood first, then?"

"Let's take a minute to consider the idea." Tonic suggests. "We might not need blood to honor the statue. What can we tell about the knight?"

Briny snorts and mutters "Oh stagnant seas!" but mulls over the statue's imagery. "There's storms, and stars." the sprite grudgingly offers.

Facet nods and continues, "Good observation! This area is Autumn distilled. And the statue is made of bronze."

"There is the wheat harvest, and the deer hunt. And the base shows a long, winding path. Maybe travel or journey?"

"Okay, so the Blood Knight is Autumn, bronze, harvest, sacrifice, storms, stars, and journeys. How does that help us get past?" Briny asks.

Facet looks at the clouds still knit grey and rainy from Briny. "Can we each offer something to match an aspect of the Blood Knight?"

Briny follows Facet's gaze and nods. "I'll offer a storm." With a quick spin, the sprite hurls Spindrift at the clouds. Giving a nasty bite and a kick, the windrabbit herds the biggest, darkest cloud down toward the statue. Spindrift nips and harries the cloud until it is rolling and black. As the storm cloud boils over the Blood Knight it lets out a mighty boom of thunder and strikes the statue's bow before scudding off toward the sea.

The space around the knight seems more open as Tonic says to the statue, "We are on a journey. My journey. And we must continue this path, for the next stage of my journey." Then Tonic puts a mug full of cinnamon-y tea at the knight's feet.

Facet takes out the half-folded Night Tent. Unscrewing a citrine star from a join between poles, the coblyn says, "Here, a star to guide you, and it was a piece of my Night Tent, too."

The space around the bronze statue has widened, and the three friends find they can easily walk around the statue and continue on the trail up the mountain; somehow the statue is simply no longer blocking their path. The incline of the path is steep here, and the air gets colder. The trio climbs with difficulty, often needing to boost each other up steep parts of the path, climbing boulders, and helping brace each other against gravity. During one boost, Tonic's pack swings around with an unfortunate *scrunch* noise, and the gnome winces, "Pretty sure we are down a cup or two now." Briny responds, "We can still use my bowls as cups, if needed!" The windrabbits do their best to help push the trio along, racing and pushing at their backs. Tonic takes out the Mighty Teaspoon Hammer and uses it like a hiking stick to balance on slopes, and to dislodge stones, making hand- and foot-holds on the nearly-vertical bits. This difficult climb last another few hours, before the path evens out.

The friends reach another leveled area and can see the next steep climb ahead. The air has turned bitter cold here, and the friends' breath comes out in cottony puffs. Briny puts on a heavy, weather-decorated deep blue peacoat, and Tonic bundles up in a quilted surtout trimmed with leaves, berries, bark, and roots (those used in tea blends, of course). This part of the mountain seems desolate; bare skeletons of plants stand starkly against the freshly fallen snow, ice crystals glitter on rocks, and icicles hang from conifers. The trail is covered with a fine hoarfrost, and each step grinds beneath their feet, with a squeaking crunch. But the thick, fluffy snow just off the trail is deep enough to build snow forts in, and several burrow entrances can be seen, dotted between trees. The landscape is rather alive, really: the holly has bright red berries showing, witch hazel has cheerful yellow blooms offering color from a high crevice, and song birds look for seeds. There is the fresh smell of evergreens, and the welcome scent of a warm fire and peppermint cocoa, a tantalizing promise of warmth and coziness somewhere in all this biting cold. Steam huddles in the travel teapot, and Turbine rustles around Facet's bronze bag. Spindrift, meanwhile, rushes and churns all around the snowy scene, howling at the world, and snapping brittle twigs off branches.

Ahead of the sprite, coblyn, and gnome is a second statue. This statue is also of a knight, this time made all of silver. The statue's armor is patterned with crystals and snowflakes. The whole thing is silver scrollwork filigree, and the gaps are filled in with small glass panes. Some of the panes are broken, but the broken panes look artistic, intentional. The knight holds up a candle in one hand, peering ahead. The other hand holds a pillow and bedroll bundle. The silver base beneath the statue has one bare shrub at the knight's feet, and nothing else. The plaque beneath the statue says "Glass Knight."

"Again?" Briny asks with frustration. "What to sacrifice this time?"

Facet considers the Glass Knight, saying, "This statue has symbols for winter, silver, fragility, clarity, desolation, rest, comfort, searching…" Looking pensive, the coblyn flips through the birchbark journal for relevant Ideas and inspirations.

"Why don't we sit down and think it through? We could all use a snack, too; our morning meal of flowers and broth was so long ago." Tonic suggests, with an affirmative tummy rumble.

The friends all sit, huddled close, and have a small meal of honey butter toast. Well, it would be toast if they had a fire. But honey butter bread is almost as good. After they eat and rest, they take some time to discuss what to do.

"I could give up my Night Ten for rest or comfort," Facet volunteers with distaste. "But then we would have nowhere to sleep safely."

Briny votes, with a laugh, to "dump a hill of snow on it, and just walk over the whole thing." The gnome and coblyn let out laughs, too.

Tonic says, "Even if there is enough snow for that plan to work, it would take ages to get it there, so lets think of other solutions, as well." Tonic taps Curious Rituals while thinking. "I know we are searching for Graemes, but I'm not leaving the journal. I think we will need it, but I don't know which bits." And looking up at the statue again, the gnome exclaims in surprise, "Well blooming buds! It's moved aside!"

As the others look, they comment in startlement, "Oh! Maybe the rest and comfort was all we needed for it?" Facet muses. The group gathers up their things and hurries to cross before the Glass Knight moves back. Again the steep path almost bests them, but nearing twilight their struggles bring them to the next knight.

At the third level area, the friends are nearly worn out. The climb has been arduous, scaling the mountain has taken most of the day, and they are unprepared for the prolonged cold they have faced. The air has warmed here, and grown more humid, as though getting ready for a rain shower. This part of the mountain is green with moss and new leaves. The trail is slick from rain and mist. A few flowers have just begun to bud and bloom, and there are butterflies flitting in the warm yellow light. The windrabbits come back out, exploring the trail, puffing butterflies, and playing sliding games on the wet path. The air smells of warm, wet earth and sweet blossoms. Dandelions, clover, violets, and jonquils bloom. A tulip magnolia tree has purple and white blossoms open and scenting the air. Tonic spots some snowdrops blooming in the shade where the ground is still frosty. Honeybees buzz around all the flowers, adding a lively humming tune to the place. Briny points out some ducklings sleeping in the sun beside a fern, and Spindrift gently rocks a hummingbird nest on a beech twig.

"Oh the weather!" Tonic says while packing extra clothing layers away, "From hot Autumn everywhere else, to the crisp it ought to be up on the mountain, then such a sharp chill, now warming moist! Briny, can you do anything? I just want the weather to decide for a minute! I'm not a fan of changing temperatures 3 or more times in a day."

As the friends now expect, ahead of them is another statue of a knight. This one is made of gold. The statue's armor is patterned to look like angry rainclouds and rushing tides; the phases of the moon trim the breastplate. Slung across the knight's back is a shield, etched with leaves of all sorts unfurling, and buds starting to open. The knight holds a pot filled with a variety of seeds in one hand, and a muddy spear held high in the other. The base of the statue is a freshly tilled field on the shore of the ocean. The plaque beneath the statue says "Storm Knight."

"Right." Briny says, adjusting the seafoam satchel and ticking off points on a hand, "The Storm Knight is Spring, gold, mud, change, garden, renewal, beginnings, tides; how do we pass this one?"

Tonic puffs air in stumped exasperation. "I don't know. We sacrificed to the Blood Knight. We rested and ate for the Glass Knight. Could we..." Facet is staring intently at the pot held by the statue, and as the gnome trails off speaking, Facet says, "Look at the seeds. Let's all do some gardening!"

The friends each choose a few seeds from the pot. Watching Tonic use the reverse end of the Mighty Teaspoon Hammer to create divots in the dirt by the statue, Briny asks, "Why don't you just dig holes with the spoon-end of your Mighty Teaspoon Hammer?"

"For planting seeds? Oh, no," Tonic's head shakes "If we were planting trees, yes. But the seeds are so small that being buried under that much dirt would smother them before they could reach the light."

"Fascinating!" Facet exclaims, writing a note in the birch bark journal. The friends all add some seeds to the divots, and Facet covers them with earth. Briny calls again on the clouds, knitting a small one into rain, and Spindrift nudging it to water the seeds.

As the seeds are nurtured with soil and water, the Storm Knight suddenly no longer blocks the path; the three friends move past, more confident than previously. As they nearly reach the next steep slope, Facet says "There must be one more statue. Each flat area is clearly representing a season, and the knight statues seem to guard that season. It seems reasonable that we found Autumn, Winter, and Spring. We just need Summer." At this utterance, the mountain growls and shudders, dusty cracks forming beneath the friends' feet. They are shaken, but cautiously continue the journey. Night is falling, yet the heat increases.

At the next flat area (after another steep, grueling, and very sweaty climb), the earth is dry and cracked, the night is oppressively hot and humid, but there is no statue, just an empty pedestal. The landscape is barren and desolate; what grasses there are, are sharp and withered. A lone figure sits to the side of the path, well-lit by the bright moon and stars. The creature's body is crisscrossed with scars and stitches, and different shades of skin. As Tonic, Briny, and Facet approach, the figure un-hunches and stands, saying despondently, "Call me Patches. Are you looking for Summer too?" The whole mountain rumbles again, and a dry layer of dust settles onto everything, "That's what I was looking for also. But don't say the name. The mountain gets really peeved." Patches finishes with a disheartened sigh.

Briny, Facet, and Tonic all blink in confusion at Patches. The many-pattered being continues, "The Knights get renamed periodically. They must be named to be given their purpose, and these names influence the coming seasons. The fourth knight has gone missing, because it has no name. Somebeing must find the Knight's name and carve it on the empty Mantle before the Wheel of the Year reaches Spring's end. The lost knight was made of copper, like the bright flame of the Summer sun." A cracking, crumbling growl shakes everybeing to the ground. "Ugh. Fine. Like the *hot* sun; better?" Patches asks the world. The group waits a moment. Seeming satisfied at a lack of further response, Patches continues, "In the past the knight has been named Plenty, Fire, Growth, Flowers, and Drought. ~ I have looked all over the mountain, but I cannot find the knight, and I don't know what to name it. Shouting words about sum... uh, er, I mean, just shouting *seasonal* words out doesn't work. Either the knight doesn't just show up when called, or I'm not using the right words."

"Can we help? You seem exhausted; kind of out of ideas. Why don't you take a break? It is only Autumn right now; you could even just go back home for a bit, and come back later refreshed?" Facet asks, brushing off sand and dust from the most recent climb, and adds, "Go home and rest, or research, before trying again?"

Patches looks surprised, a greenish patch of skin raising high over a brown eye, and the thick stitching between a yellow piece and a purplish bit of flesh making a triangle over a blue eye. "Have none of you looked back yet?" Patches goes on with some pity, "You chose this path. The only way out is forward, new choices. You don't get a do-over."

Gnome, sprite, and coblyn slowly turn to look down the path behind them. "Oh," they all breathe. There is no path behind them. Where before the path was blocked by the statues and thick, impassible forest and underbrush, behind them there is nothing. Like the way back just decided to stop existing, or a lazy storyteller couldn't decide how to describe yet another challenge.

After a moment staring behind them in amazement, Tonic opens Graeme's journal at random for inspiration, and reads with a slight sneeze, "You can always leave. You don't need anyone's permission, but if it helps, you have mine..."

"That's actually pretty comforting," Facet says.

"What? How does it apply? There is no path!" Briny points out, while trying to brush off dust that is now caked-on to clothes and satchel from the mist and sweat.

"Okay," Facet continues "There is no path behind us; we made a choice and can't go back to the start and choose something else. But we can always leave. We just have to choose going forward in a different way."

"Yes!" Tonic pipes up, "That's what Graemes says. Whether it is a job, a hairstyle, a relationship, or a meal, you can always choose to change it. Leave, choose something different.'"

Patches is astonished, and stands still for several minutes, with multi-length, multi-hued hair tangling in the sandy wind. Just as Briny asks, "Are you okay?" Patches re-animates. Then with a joyful whoop, Patches dances toward the statue base. Using a powerful leap, Patches picks up the shield that had been leaning against the statue's base, and proceeds to slide down the side of the mountain, letting out an enthusiastic "Thank youuu...!" Soon exhilarated whoops, hollers, and screams echo back up the mountain. They mostly seem cheerful, and only occasionally terrified.

"I'm glad that was helpful." Tonic says with a small cough, still rather shocked "The mountainside is pretty steep, but apparently not impossible. I guess Patches never considered that leaving was always a choice you can make?"

"Yes, I think a lot of beings forget that after making a choice, you can still choose something different. It is always good to be reminded that you can leave." Facet agrees, while trying to face away from the hot, abrasive night wind. And generally failing, as the wind manages to scrub at them from every angle.

Briny nods, like a wave at low-tide, "Knowing we can leave is good, but I want to find the missing Knight so that we can make it to the Tree Beyond the Garden. Any ideas?"

The sprite, coblyn, and gnome try to think of the next step in finding the missing knight, but they find concentration difficult with the searing night's dry heat and scouring dusty wind. Briny feels parched and looks thinned-out. Every-which-way they turn still blows rough grit into their faces, and there is no protection from the constant coating of grime. Finally, the trio circles together with arms linked and heads bent in, to block the wind for each other.

"Okay," Facet asks while spitting out sand, "What epitomizes summer? Oh, blasting stones..."

At the mention of 'summer' the bright sky itself shakes to fractures, and the mountain powders to dry, scorching dust. Everything sinks down some into the fine, sucking mountain of sand.

"Blistering buds! It is boiling hot!" Tonic yells in fear. Reaching toward Briny and Facet, the gnome tries to pull them out of the sinking sand.

Steam hops out of the travel teapot to help, blowing mightily (like gentle puffs of air). Spindrift and Turbine join in, but all the windrabbits' efforts only seem to shift the friends further into the sand. Facet's ankles are locked fast, and Tonic is buried nearly to the knees. Briney's long, thin legs have fallen surprisingly deep into the burning sand; the sprite feels wrung-out and ill. Facet pauses to figure out a plan (could they somehow build the sand minerals into a shelter?) and Tonic uses short, powerful arms to try to reach Briny, hoping to help free the sallow-looking sprite.

Briny angrily struggles to be released, feeling the tie to water and tides leaking away into the dehydrating dirt. The sprite's seafoam satchel is thrown free with a sharp crack during the trio's thrashing attempt to get free. Briny is sweating and scared, and quickly going murky and gaunt. The desiccating sand greedily sucks away all the moisture around, and the already-parched Briny swiftly dries out: fading from thin to foggy, then wisps curl away. Like a magic trick, the sprite's fingertips disappear. All rainbow shimmers and curling waves are gone as Briny's foggy limbs turn misty, then barely hazy. Soon the sprite is only starlight twinkling reflections on scattering vapors.

In less than a moment, Briny has dissipated.

Chapter 10: Continuing

Staring in silent shock, Facet and Tonic don't know what to do. This was supposed to be a fun, lighthearted quest to find an often-absent mentor; a chance to see some new things. A sweet romp of a Wanderlust to rejuvenate their spirits! How can their friend be gone? So fast, without warning?

Facet screams and rummages for tools, Bits, Devices, anything that might help. Tonic tries to dig into the burning grit and dust, looking for their friend; maybe Briny just slipped into the sand. Spindrift snuffles disconsolately at the dirt and satchel.

Tonic and Facet lash out in a slurry of words, yelling grief-stricken accusations to eternity and each other. The words pile and clash together: "What do we do now?! Why didn't you act faster? How do we get Briny back?! Where do we go?! How could Briny be GONE? You should have known!

How can this happen?! That's our FRIEND! You should have saved Briny! Bad things can't happen to *us*! Why couldn't I DO anything?! Why didn't you *help*?!"

Although the sand still burns and scrapes into their legs, they holler desolation and loneliness at each other, crying for the unfairness (the windrabbits hide from the out-pouring of pain). Still stuck in the aggregation of sand, the friends fight and struggle. The burning, gritty, unceasing wind whips at them and slowly wears their anger and shock away, carrying the tiny particles of emotion far away on the air currents, and eventually leaving gnome and coblyn worn out and defeated.

Once all is quiet again, the friends having exhausted their fighting, and only the ceaseless, stirring susurrus of the wind remains, Facet and Tonic slump down on the hot, sandy ground. The mountain has leveled out from the air currents carrying away, and sifting smooth, the sandy soil. Pre-dawn light glows on the horizon; all the shock and shouting means Facet never even thought to put up the Night Tent, and neither friend has slept. Then, as gentle as the breath before a storm, Facet hears the delicate trickle of sand shifting. Tonic points at the depression where Briny had been, and Facet and Tonic watch the grit shift and swirl in its own eddies of air. The faintest whisper of breeze, like the soughing of a single, irritated leaf, says "Oh, pond scum! This desiccated sand is miserable and greedy," in exactly Briny's stormy bluster.

Briny, an invisible rush of air, pulls free from the grasp of the abandoned Summer's sand. "I'm a water sprite, but I am made of tides and *storms*. I am partially of the air; I'm the weather, and no nasty, grumpy, *pouting* grains of dehydrating dirt will stop me!" Nothing more than a darkly breezing whisper, Briny's vehemence is still blatant. "I need a proper map to get myself back. It takes too much effort to remain myself as just a breeze."

Tonic and Facet cheer to know their friend is there,

although they cannot see the sprite. The sun is up by now, though barely, and glaring harshly at the dry mountain. Facet croaks with a throat sore from shouting, "Briny, I've got just the Idea." Turbine nudges open Facet's birchbark journal and kick-flips the pages until Facet says, "There. I did some map sketches at Nightshade's. It's enough for a Sudden Idea, when in need. We will build you a map back to yourself." A brand-new Sudden Idea hops up from the birchbark, all shiny metallic like a compass rose, and scurries to Facet's hand. Gathering the coblyn's whispered words, the little Sudden Idea rustles over to the astonished Tonic and waits. Facet says, "Think of our Sprite. Who is Briny? The words will be a map." Tonic stutters words through cracked lips, and the tiny map Idea flutters into the space where Briny's breeze is.

The sprite swirls the Sudden Idea up and laughs with whispered joy, "This is perfect, my friends. Thank you." Then rising high in transparent spirals of air, Briny floats in nimbus clouds, pulling in their vapors. Then the sprite starts calling out the words from Tonic and Facet, and it sounds like bated stillness and screaming torrents, "I was the wind and the ocean. I was the wind and the ocean... "

A huge crack of lightning surges through the air, etching Briny in rainbow crackles of electricity. All three windrabbits race toward the sea, snapping and harrying a Storm Herd of black clouds before them. The sprite's chant continues, more screaming torrent now than bated stillness, and the Storm Herd thunders toward the flattened mountain. Rain pours down all around.

Briny says with surprise in a low voice, like the barest rustle of raindrops on leaves, "I was the wind and the ocean, torn apart, then my friends built a map, back to me..." The invisible sprite stands on the edge of the eroding cliff, looking at the wild rain mixing with foaming surf and seaspray; everything is soaked and pulled about by the storm.

Briny's voice crashes and fades like a storm-tossed boat on wave swells, then sounds more like wind soughing and wuthering. The conjured storm pauses, then builds according to the sprite's map-words:

I Was the Wind and the Ocean.
I stood on the edge of sadness,
Looking at the chasm beneath me.

Thoroughly drenched with the high-altitude precipitations, and still lightly illuminated, the water sprite laughs and climbs a cumulus rope back to the once-barren swath of now-muddy land; the feel of the cloud-rope is silky and cool.

On the balcony of despair,
The wind played with my hair,
Tossing it about my face.

Facet and Tonic are still stuck in the sand, and they soon become completely mired as the rains keep falling, churning the mountain of rubble to mud.

Then it picked me up,
Swirled me to places my mind had yet to see.

The windrabbits are still driving clouds toward Briny, and those Storm Herd rushes again, roiling nearer. The sprite smells the ocean's salt waves and the fresh-metallic scent of the Storm Herd.

I ran atop the ocean,
The sea-spray in my clothes,

The sky is black with boiling clouds, rain is lashing down,

and the cracking thud of the heavy hooves of the Storms spark electricity that sears sand into glistening glass. Briny hears the roaring crash of clouds and waves all around. To the coblyn and gnome, it seems the world might break, and never be calm again Tonic manages to get a grip on the Mighty Teaspoon hammer and uses it as a leverage point.

Waves pushing at my frame,
Begging me to join them.
So I did.

As Tonic and Facet help pull each other free of the sticky earth, the Storm Herd's snapping, rumbling clouds continue with a passion. Facet calls out, trying to be heard above the rising storm, "The tea leaves, Tonic! Do you remember what you read in them? Is this when we need Briny's ferocious emotions?"

I flung out my arms
With my head held high,
And laughed at the Great Unknown,

"Yes!' Tonic agrees with an overused voice, "I think you are right! And the missing season; it has caused a land of desolation and death. I think Summer is the grave enemy." Turning toward the sprite, with the land in tremors from the mention of Summer, Tonic shouts to be heard above the storm "Briny! Is that the hidden poem?!" Great chunks of sandy mountain sheer off and slough away all around the friends. The sprite remembers the taste of the tea and focuses on being here with friends.

Then fell backwards into the foam.
I was the Wind and the Ocean

The sudden wind and waves from Briny's chanted map

further wash the mountain away. In surprise the sprite stills, uttering the last lines of the map.

And I laughed.

Briny's new skin shines like river stones and angry tidal pools. The sprite laughs in waves, falling onto the ground, exhausted.

Looking around, Facet and Tonic find the mountain has totally worn away, into a flat, sandy shore. The far-off ocean that was beyond the mountain is now at their feet, not so far off, and lapping seafoam at their toes. The wild, violent hurricane quickly diminishes, and the Storm Herd disperses. Clouds of summersweet flowers grow in abundance where Briny was consumed by the harsh earth of the fourth season. The flowers' scent is a fresh, sweet, woody smell, something like a blend of honeysuckle, rose, and clove. The buttery dawn light is friendly on the newly-made beach.

Exhausted, gnome and coblyn help their more-exhausted friend walk, while asking concerned questions. "Briny! That was astounding!" Tonic gushes.

"How did you do all that? I never knew you could exist without your water! We really thought you were...gone..." Facet trails off.

"Are you okay?" Briney asks the sprite, while giving a big hug. "Your song was glorious! Where did it come from?"

Briny smiles sleepily and replies, "Thank you both. I am okay, just worn out. Surviving while my water and storms are separated is *miserable*; it hurts like blazes. I'm so glad you could give me a map back to myself! And that might not even have been enough without the lightning strike. I'm so *tired*." Briney's yawn echoes like surf in a cavern.

Facet guides the group toward some shade where they can rest, as Briny continues dreamily, "The map-song was perfect. Like music playing me into existence. It was the rhythm of a brilliant, clear night on the seaside; the waves crashing onto the beach in a joyful, powerful way and jellies glowing blue along the crests of the waves; the stars shine crystalline while bright meteors race across the black silk arc of the night sky."

Wading through a sea of fireflies, the drained friends help each other into the shade, near the plinth where the absent statue belongs. Tonic pulls over large palm and banana leaves to use as pallets. Facet observes, "We will have to find the missing knight later. Briny needs to recover, and you and I are beyond weary from the night's exertions too." As the sun rises higher in the sky, white clouds are scudding across the blue above, there is smooth sand below, and the day seems to promise seagulls playing and interesting shells to be found; the trio rests amid the seagrasses on the warm, inviting beach. Steam, Spindrift, and Turbine all frisk in the waves; Spindrift brings Briny some rainbow bracelets from the tideline. You can almost smell ice cream cones and the new-plastic of freshly inflated beach floats. A sandcastle sits just off to one side, two crabs industriously building up the towers. Soft green grasses coat nearby hills, ready for barefoot races. The beach is peaceful, and the stillness just waits to be full of friends, and fun, and long, warm days full of kites and laughter. The three friends drowsily rest in the shade.

Sometime later, gnome and coblyn are motivated by their grumbling tummies. Briny dozes on the leaf pallet and damp sand, with toes gently patted by the ocean waves. The sprite's skin continues to glisten like smooth stones and shadow like hidden pools; mist and clouds seem to crawl across Briny, but Facet and Tonic can't ever quite see them when they look directly at their friend. Something unusual is happening, and they fervently hope Briny will be alright. Tonic makes some energizing tea, noting that there isn't much left in the provisions they packed. While the tea steeps, Facet assists the gnome in looking for edible plants nearby. Tonic points out a clump of dulse and nori seaweed to Facet, while gathering a bundle of unexpected cattails beside a marshy pond. "Put those in the oakcorn basket, they will make a good meal; I think we will need to rest here a day while Briny recovers. Oh, rosehips and some blackberries! And curly dock!" Tonic exclaims and adds the ripe berries and fat green leaves to the oakcorn as they walk back to the sleeping sprite. "Some of the plants ought not be in season, but I think they are from the seasons on the mountain. Grab that glasswort, too, Facet!" Coblyn and gnome prepare the plants and watch over their recuperating friend. After the food is ready, they gently wake Briny up enough for a snack, and the weary trio eat. It has been a long day and night, full of physical stress and emotional turmoil.

Briny is quickly back asleep, recovery powered by cattail sausages and seaweed salad. Facet rests and sips tea with Tonic. "What is the next step?" the gnome wonders aloud with a yawn. "How do we finish the task of finding the missing knight?"

The windrabbits kick up sand and push flowers high into the salty air while the friends drowsily try to think up an answer, relaxing in the warming comfort of the sand. Still asleep, Briny reaches out, and they all hold hands, like sleeping otters. The sleeping sprite gives a contented sigh.

Shortly, Facet snorts awake from an inspiring dream, and suggests aloud, "I think we need to find the essence of the season. All the others were named for some part of their core. What has the fourth season been for us? Or what do we want it to be?" Sleeping in the sun and shade on the shore, Briny happily murmurs something that might have been 'relax,' or might have been 'rest,' or possibly even 'recover' (some insist the word was 'berries,' but as no one can say definitively, you shall have to decide for yourself what you think it was). Tonic and Facet can't tell, as both are already back asleep.

The trio sleep through the day, and thus they don't notice the tide come in, or how it carries them along on their leaf pallets; the friends are still holding hands like otters, which keeps them together, and the windrabbits gently brace the trio along. When Briny, Facet, and Tonic all wake at dawn the next morning, the friends find themselves washed somewhere new.

"Where are we?" Briny wonders, tucking the tuckered-out windrabbits into pack, bag, and satchel.

"I'm not sure. This isn't where we fell asleep." Tonic replies, looking at the forest just beyond the sand dunes.

Facet points to an island in the distance, "Look! I see four tall statues on that island; I think the Summer Knight must finally be named." The friends pause, full of trepidation, but no rumbling or shaking comes. "Whew. It seems the Knight is found! I wonder who found it? A shame we made all that effort, but slept through the finale. At least the work got completed, though! ...I hope wherever this is, that we are closer to the Tree Beyond the Garden."

Briny points out plump, ripe dewberries growing in a neat line, leading like a trail straight to the forest. "I think we go to the woods. I'm pretty sure this path is a thank you from the knights. I think we must have been helpful in Summer's recovery."

Looking dubious for a moment, Tonic agrees, "To the woods, then." While gathering dewberries in the oakcorn basket, Tonic and Briny list ideas. Facet takes notes as they travel beyond the dewberries and further down the path:

"Enjoy dewberries, finish the last blackberries. Bring chalk, mark the trees; don't let the forest turn us around. Avoid known dangerous plants; no more spikes, poison sap, or itchy rashes. Spill the rosehips. Untangle branches; sometimes this requires a knife or the Teaspoon Hammer. Fall into and find a huge hole; try to find hole first next time, and avoid the falling part. Discover a hidden clearing to camp in; yay! Night Tent worked perfectly, was able to put it away before first light. Realize there is no food to break our fast today; must have lost the last in the hole. Also 2 of Tonic's cups are broken, and one of Briny's bowls is all shards. Follow the winding trail up the hill and out the other side of the woods. Be hungry and exhausted. Spot a village in the distance! Argue."

Chapter 11: Marginalia

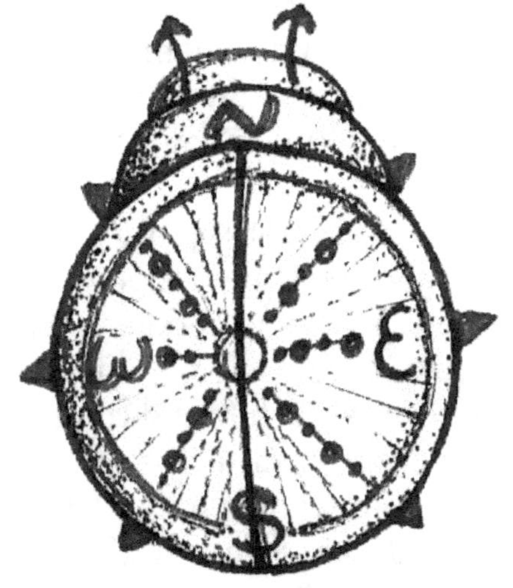

Once out the other side of the woods, coblyn, sprite,
and gnome walk for some time, discussing their adventure.
Falling into a hole is agreed to be a low point; sleeping in the
Night Tent on the winding trail was definitely the highlight.
Facet consults some notes, "We need to find the twisting
village. It is supposed to shift and change every time you
observe it. The Tree Beyond the Garden is in the woods
just past their meadow. Getting through the village will be
difficult, though. Any thoughts or plans? I have been caring
for the Sudden Idea about maps that helped you, Briny. I
want to see if it can help us traverse the shifting streets."

Briny is quick to speak up, "From what Vellum said, there
is a creek that goes around and through the village; I think
we can use that to bypass the challenging Village of Twist."

Tonic isn't so sure. "I think we are going to need
some local knowledge. The Village of Twist is part of the

Marginalia. I don't think it can easily be defeated or snuck around. But Vellum said people live there, so somebeing must be able to help guide us!"

With a stormy temper, the water sprite argues, "We can't just ask. What would we tell them? If they guard the Lintel to the World's Between, they aren't just going to take us to the Tree Beyond the Garden! And remember how concerned the panel was at your Conclusion? I don't think we can just tell people that you are a Wildling. They might purposely leave us lost and trapped there!"

"Those are valid concerns." the garden gnome agrees "I think we could find a way through, though. Facet is great at explaining things, and inspiring people to join in. I'm sure if we ask, it will work."

A disagreement grows, each friend thinking their way is the only way, and no compromise is reached. After lengthy discussion, Briny says "I'm going to try it my way and you try it yours," and storms ahead in a huff. Tonic looks at Facet, who shrugs in agreement. It seems they have finally come to a consensus; they will each try their own way, see who gets to the Tree first, and then help the others reach it. All of their discourse means the trio arrives at the labyrinthine village on their map sooner than they expect; mist is clinging to everything. It's often difficult to notice your journey when emotions are high.

"Oh, whoa. Here is the twisted village." Facet quavers, pointing to two signs that loom out of the thick fog. One sign is made of wood that is dark and squeezed by vines, it is carved with "Village of Twist" in curly letters; the other sign is a tall grey stone, which is carved with loops and whorls and says "Twisting Village." Both signs point at the village entrance, which can just barely be seen through the thick, blanketing fog. The trio moves closer to the village, trying to see what the village actually looks like. Peering over the slate stones of the houses, the somber shining metals, the deep red color of the street bricks, the bright glass windows, and the heavy dark wood doors and fences, Facet remarks, "The dark and bright patterns must reflect light so that it is hard to see where you are going; like tricks with mirrors." Turbine huddles down in the coblyn's bronze bag, and the Sudden Ideas timidly peek out of the birchbark journal.

Briny cuddles Spindrift and comments, "The mist here never goes away. I can tell from the way the weather moves. The mist will shift, but the air stays moist; it only turns thicker into fog, or back into wisps of mist. It must be miserable to see anything clearly."

Tonic gulps and puts Steam back into the teapot, with the lid firmly closed. "Okay. Are we all ready to get through this Marginalia maze village?" Doubting whether they should split up, Tonic watches Briny walk toward the creek, singing to the current, and sees Facet eagerly follow one of the Sudden Ideas around to the far side of the Village wall, before both are obscured by the ever-shifting fog.

"Well," the gnome says to a nearby rosemary bush, "We are at the Marginalia, we are so close. But we are separated. Briny trusts the creek and windrabbit to lead a safe water route. Facet is inspired by a Sudden Idea. I really wish we were together."

Walking through the gates and into Twist Village, Tonic looks at the red brick lane and dark slate buildings nearby and feels lost among the shifting streets and abundant alleyways; light glints and hides, mist curls and creeps over everything. After a few nervous attempts to ask for help Tonic realizes that the villagers are mostly on busy errands of their own. The residents of Twisting Village aren't exactly rude, but also not very helpful when approached by a strange gnome. While standing in a park green, and trying to determine which way to go, and feeling terribly turned around, Tonic spots a cheerful figure chatting with some villagers and allowing a weary butterfly to warm in the sun from a perfectly-still hand. Something about the care the villager shows to the butterfly gives Tonic a good feeling. The tea gnome goes over to say hello and see if this villager can help navigate the way to the Tree Beyond the Garden.

Offering their name as "River Brindle, of Okashi Street" the villager is tall and lithe, with large hazel eyes, beautiful wavy orange hair, and black stripes. And the wonderful thing is that although the gnome is feeling lost and nervous in the constantly-new, peek-a-boo village, there is someone offering to help. Tonic remembers dire warnings from stories and myths, and briefly fears that this new friend might not be as genuine as they seem. However, the duo keep to bright, populous places, and this stripey new friend is kind and considerate of all Tonic says and asks. The gnome decides to trust their gut, and takes advice from Graeme's journal, "Many stories are told as cautionary tales; they are created to try to keep us safe. But often they also make us fearful, so we forget that anyone is capable of being helpful. Talk to those you meet; most will be kind. Trust yourself when you think something is hinky."

Tonic decides to follow the stripy River, and stays alert in case anything seems wrong. As they travel, "Never a straight path in the village" River Brindle explains, they talk about life here, and life in the Teapot. The village is too far from any professors, so they don't have Craft Courses or Conclusions the way Facet, Briny, and Tonic did. "We largely learn from apprenticeship and errors." River Brindle gives a cheerful laugh. "The young are encouraged to try things, and get them wrong, and when we find skills we enjoy, we go apprentice with someone to improve ourselves. I myself have apprenticed at many places, and I've had a few apprentices too. Getting things wrong is how I got so many patches in my vest. I keep fixing it to remind me of all I've tried and learned." River explains with a smile, pointing out stitches and patches in various shades on the black tweed vest.

They go up streets, and down gardens, under stairs, and across bridges, sharing stories and comfortable silences all the way. In this unsettling place, Tonic is relieved to share stories of the tea garden, of comforting things like blending and smashing, and of hopes and hurdles for the future. The gnome feels good talking about things with confidence, in this place of shifting certainty. River Brindle is delighted to let the enthusiastic gnome talk and explain the intricacies of a passion for tea, and life back at the teapot.

The journey through the Village of Twist is dizzying, disorienting, and not short, so River Brindle has them take several breaks. Tonic feels comfortable with River Brindle, but has a difficult time dealing with the ever-changing streets and buildings. The gnome fidgets abundantly, dealing with the discomfort of the unusual place by letting out the unsettled feelings in physical jitters, taps, and cloth twists. Once, when feeling anxious, Tonic unconsciously pets River Brindle's tail as they sit eating lunch at the Temper and Scale pub.

After a while, the gnome realizes the faux pas, and looks at River Brindle in embarrassment. "Oh no! I didn't realize I was holding your tail...I'm so sorry! I've been terribly worried, and I didn't ask..."

River Brindle cuts in saying "It's okay. It's not a bother. If it helps you feel better, then please continue. Sometimes you need to hold a friend's hand, or tail, when you are scared." Smiling, River Brindle keeps talking until Tonic is ready to continue traveling. They start walking with Tonic still holding onto River Brindle's tail like a security blanket or worry stone.

They continue their journey through the village, until they are stopped by a grass-tufted villager who asks River Brindle with disgust "Why would you let somebeing hold your tail?!"

The two villagers seemed to know each other, as River Brindle responds with familiarity. As they talk, Tonic begins to fear being left in this unknown place, far from friends. The serene River Brindle calmly retorts "My friend needs help, and I do not mind. Have you even a tail to be held? How do you know it's terrible if you've never tried it?"

Rebuffed, the villager stands wordless and grumpy. River Brindle and Tonic walk on through the maze of the Marginalia village. They travel far, and double back, and sometimes have to run to keep up with the wily, changing path. Eventually they come to the edge of town, to an open meadow. River Brindle says "Here is your destination; my journey goes elsewhere, my friend. Just look for the violet-filled hollow in the ground. It was once a well-traveled mound but is now only a forgotten depression in the forest beyond the meadow."

Tonic replies "Thank you. Can I have a hug before you go?" With a fierce hug, River Brindle hands over a parcel of cheese and bread, and asks "Are you alright now? Have everything you need for your adventure?" Tonic nods doubtfully. Noting the new friend's uncertainty, River Brindle reaches into a vest pocket. Handing over a soft, toy moth the tall, striped friend adds, "Here, you might need something comforting to hug on your journey, and my tail has to come with me. Travel safe my friend. Well met and meet again."

Tonic tucks the plush moth into a petal pocket of their overalls, and replies, "Well met and meet again!" as the helpful new friend heads back into the village. Once River has left, the gnome looks around and suddenly realizes that the plan (reach the end of the village, then go back to find the others) was a terrible one. The gnome looks down at Steam sniffing the grasses and asks the windrabbit, "How can we possibly back-track our own path to find them on theirs? Where would they even be? We chose different routes...
That plan didn't make as much sense as we thought." Tonic slumps with regret.

Watching Steam play in the meadow grasses, Tonic
perks up; inviting the windrabbit to help, Tonic sends
Steam off to find Spindrift and Turbine. "Didn't Briny say
that windrabbits would help us stay in touch?" Tonic muses
aloud, fervently hoping the windrabbits can find each other.
Steam curls up high, like puffs from a giant kettle, floating
and spiraling above the treetops, and over the village. Then
Steam whistles a song loudly to the other two windrabbits.
After an anxious wait, and a few more whistles, there is an
answering hissing from the left, and a splashing from the
right. Upon hearing this, Steam dances a happy, curling,
twirling jig in the air. With quick, piping whistles the
windrabbit rejoins the bewildered Tonic. "What is it, Steam?
Did you find the others? Where are they?" Shortly, Tonic's
joy soars; around the corner Turbine tumbles ahead of Facet,
glittering like gem dust in the air, and from across the stream
Spindrift surges forward, leading Briny on paws splashing
like flecks of seafoam.

Chapter 12: Stories

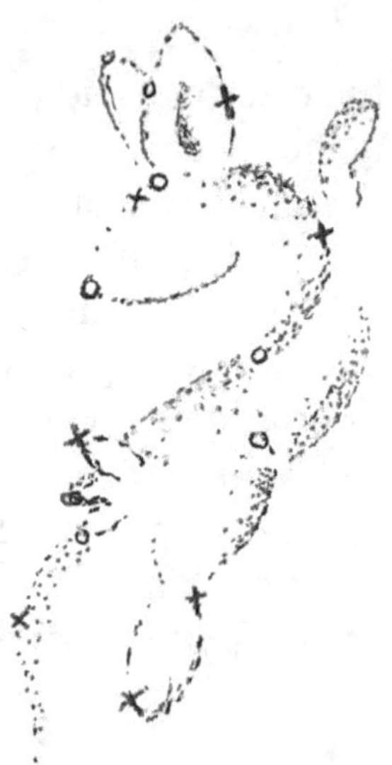

With Facet, Briny, and Tonic all reunited, evening is arriving. All three friends want to share their stories, but agree to get settled for the night first. They arrange a camping spot, set out dinner, and once it is dark enough, they set up the Night Tent.

"...Wait a moment more," cautions Facet, watching the sun's light on the horizon, "Just a biiit longer..." Briny impatiently starts to reach for the folded star in Facet's bronze bag, saying "It's dark enough! I want to tell our adventure tales!" However, the coblyn shoves the emerging star box back into the bag and looks accusingly at Briny's jam-covered hand. Tonic chuckles, "Briny, we won't all FIT in a squashed sandwich! Let Facet set it up, and we can gather some food; I'm pretty sure that's biscuitroot over in that rocky patch, and I think we will find skirret, sourwood, groundnut, and salsify over there near the pines."

The trio hug and joke and laugh as they go about their

tasks. Turbine assists with starting a fire, and Steam helps find tasty plants. Spindrift stays in the Seafoam Satchel and rests from a grueling day of trying to un-lose their way through the creek. Once they are all settled with the Night Tent set up (one corner looking a bit saggy and blotched with jam), and all eating their meal of roasted veggies, bread, and cheese, the friends are eager to share their stories.

Briny goes first, the tale tumbling out like tidal waves: "You were right, Tonic. The creek is part of the village, and it did not allow me to swim my way around the Marginalia's twisting. I had a terrible rough time. The creek was never where it should be, and sometimes it wasn't even a creek or a stream! I would swim forward into open water, only to bash into impossible rocks and muddy banks. Everything was disorienting and uncomfortable, and I hated feeling alone. Every time I thought I was making progress, I kept finding myself back beyond the wall, or halfway out in the forest! Once I even found myself in the ocean; I had to swim a current that was hidden in a subaquatic cave to keep up with that twist. The stream did not like my affinity for water and it had to pull a lot of tricks to keep me turned around! Everyway I faced was upstream current. Spindrift could barely keep up with the flickering speed of twists. Skidding along the surface as fast as a freshening wind, that windrabbit almost got twisted to places without me! I had nearly made it into the middle of the village, when I came to some shallows lush with cattails and thick with mountain laurel. The fight to get there was exhausting, as whatever way I went, I was fighting strong currents. The place was gorgeous, though, just like The Shallows at home! Spindrift sniffed a laurel bloom floating in the stream, just as the place twisted again. I was horrified! I barely caught a hindfoot as I felt the waters changing, and Spindrift ended up stretched thin across several waters. Poor thing was barely a puff for a while. As soon as I could, I started to collect Spindrift up into my arms, calling the fierce little Gale to me across the wide winds and waters. It took forever, I was worn out from trying to stay still in the shifting river, but every moment Spindrift was stretched meant another twist and a further stretch of the windrabbit. I gathered as swiftly as I could, coiling the rabbit up and gathering as much breeze into my arms as I could; I think Spindrift lost a bit of an ear, but it will heal." Briny gently pets the sleeping rabbit in the satchel and goes on, "Once I had Spindrift together I just slumped against the riverbank and stayed still, cradling the little windrabbit as the world twisted around us. I think I slept that way for a while. That's where we were when Spindrift heard Steam singing. I'm so glad I was already holding the rabbit, or I never would have been able to keep up! I'm so relieved to be with you both again. I missed you, my friends." Briny finishes the story with a smile and a friendly hand-squeeze.

Facet's story is next, of using a Sudden Idea and getting help from some Bits and Pieces. "I didn't think we could just ASK for help, and I really wanted to use the Sudden Idea about maps! I opened to a fresh page in my birchbark journal, and started mapping what I could see of the town. The Sudden Idea helped orient me, and I kept track of where I'd traveled with my stratigraphy skirt. I walked around part of the outside of the Village, but the edges kept mutating, and didn't properly match up. I was sometimes on one side, sometimes another, but never going where I wanted to. The Sudden Idea worked so hard to help me, I even named it! Meet Maplet." Facet takes out a small snail with a shell marked like a treasure map, and a small rose compass on top. "I took a break to breathe and assess my map pages; I have pieces of maps crammed-in all over multiple pages. It's a mess! Look!" The coblyn brandishes the scraps and journal pages to illustrate the point. "So, while resting, I was reorganizing my birchbark journal, and also my bronze bag, when I found a Bit hidden in the bottom! I have a Piece in my pocket, and I think I focused on that for a while; I remember the light changing. It might have been night, because I got out the folded-up Night Tent and used it as a glowing star to see by. I was eventually able to construct a Useful Device, which was reenergizing for me! Unfortunately, the Useful Device I created wasn't much help with the *specific* problem of navigating the Village of Twist; it allows me to see further, but as the village keeps changing and shifting, seeing distant things wasn't really pertinent. It just made me more aware of how lost I was in regard to my mission," Facet says while showing the crammed map pages and Useful Device to the friends. After Briny and Tonic get to examine the maps and murmur appreciatively over the Useful Device, Facet packs them back away in the bronze bag, knowing the Useful Device will be helpful later.

Tonic shares the story of befriending River Brindle, and getting guided through the ever-changing village of Twist.

(*Much later, Tonic learns that River Brindle journeyed far away, and the gnome realized they weren't likely to meet again. Tonic makes a note in Graeme's journal, "Although having friends too far away to visit may be sad, it is good to have met them. Some friends are deeply important to us even when we only see them for a short time. Being far away doesn't end a friendship." While writing in the journal, Tonic wished they had exchanged some way to send letters to each other and adds, "A happy thing to look forward to from a friend is a much-needed delight.")

The three friends are happy to be reunited and get some rest. Although they aren't entirely certain how much time they spent trying to get around and through the Twisting Village, the trio do all agree that they are once again *tired*. The next morning, Tonic, Facet, and Briny are all together, and the Lintel is close; the friends feel full of hope. "River Brindle said the Tree Beyond the Garden is just past this meadow, in the woods there." Tonic points. "So after we break our fast, we'll be on our way!"

With the sun already up as the friends finish breakfast, Facet nearly manages to get the Night Tent mostly folded up again. Rather than a hand-sized glowing star, it looks more like a pillow-sized moldy sandwich, but at least it is mostly put away. Briny quips, "I like camping, but I think I'm bad at being up out of the tent before dawn." To which Tonic adds, "I like how my teapot never gets squishy if I get up late!" The friends laugh while Tonic uses the Mighty Teaspoon Hammer to put dirt on the fire, and Briny finds water to do the washing up.

The morning light warms up the wide meadow, evaporating dew, and waking the flowers. It promises to be a lovely morning, and they are almost at the end of their journey. Walking hand-in-hand-in-hand the three friends cavort across the meadow. "You know what?" Tonic asks aloud, "I feel much lighter. I don't have the urgency I felt at the start of the Wanderlust. I've traveled some, I've been to new places, met new people, I even helped the Season Knights! I think I'm coming around to the idea of going home again."

The meadow, which had looked so short, seems to just keep unrolling in front of them. The friends soon slow their cavort to a calm walk, and eventually a puzzled plod.

Sweaty, slightly confused, and appearing to be about halfway through a meadow that should only be 20 paces across, the coblyn, sprite, and gnome pause to assess their situation. "How long is this meadow?!" Briny exclaims as the trio rest.

Looking towards the woods on the far side, Facet points across the meadow, "Is that the Lintel up ahead? I think I see something!" The friends turn and see a colored dome in the distance. Excited, the trio run and tumble toward the apparently not-too-distant dome, and the windrabbits race behind them, rushing wind at their backs.

Chapter 13: Weathervane

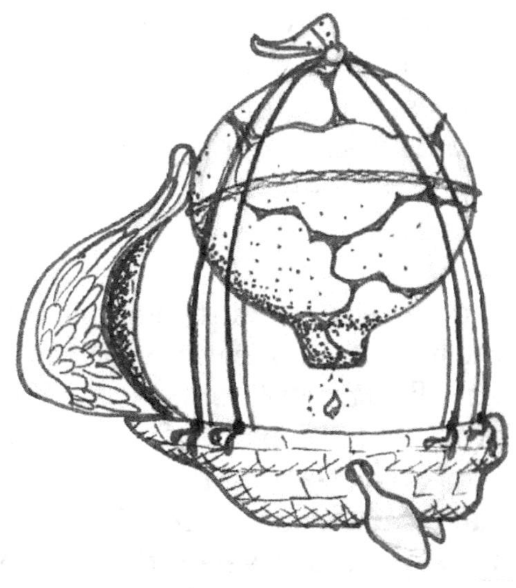

Actually approaching the dome takes some time, but not so long as the trio feared in this strange, scrunched-up meadow. Upon closer sight, the unexplained bulge is a large, round, puffy, rainbow-kaleidoscope of color; and it seems to be inflating. A figure bustles loudly behind the growing bubble, and there is a constant roaring-hum of a noise happening inside the dome. As Briny, Tonic, and Facet approach the scene, the windrabbits rush up and over the bright cloth curve, twirling and snuffling playfully. A hearty, "Hullo! Fairwinds, little friends," booms from the other side of the dome, where the three windrabbits went.

Rounding to the far side, the coblyn, sprite, and gnome see a cheerful, busy figure giving bits of sand to the windrabbits (the airy lagomorphs are happily crunching up the tiny particles). The stranger is a bird with a small beak, who is wearing spectacles and a light blue cravat.

Tonic calls "Greetings and hospitality!" while Briny waves and Facet peers at the woven room next to the figure.

Looking up in surprise, the stranger greets the three friends. "Hullo there! Are these windrabbits your friends? They are wonderful!" Flapping a wing in salutation, the stranger continues, "Call me Weathervane. Have you ever worked on a hot air balloonship before? I could use some help with mine. We lost some things during a spot of nasty weather recently, so Compass went to fetch some supplies, but my dear twin set out ages ago! We are the Nightjar twins; have you heard of us? We write and reenact our explorations!"

The friends stare uncertainly at the enthusiastic figure. Noticing the hesitation, Weathervane continues, "Weathervane Poorwill Nightjar? Compass Frogmouth Nightjar? The famous twins, exploring by land and air? ... no? Well, no matter! You are in for a treat, because you now are able to make our acquaintances! I travel the skies by balloonship, and Compass traverses the land. We put on performances of our most astounding adventures, so all may know of lands far flung and learn of the wonders within them!"

"Do you need any help?" Facet offers. "I've not worked on a hot air balloonship before, but I'm pretty good at making things. I think if you tell us what to do, we could follow directions."

"Splendid!" Weathervane crows with enthusiasm. "I appreciate all the help you can give. Here, just hold this rope," the bird-creature hands a rope to Facet, "And, if you would help pull the basket upright; perhaps your Teaspoon Hammer will help give leverage," Weathervane continues, motioning at Tonic, "And, could you have the windrabbits assist in filling the balloon? We will have this set in no time!"

The group works hard following Weathervane's instructions, pushing and pulling and straightening and twisting all the bits that need adjusting, until the hot air balloonship is filled, and ready to take off. While waiting for Compass to return, the friends ask Weathervane to share stories of the twins' travels.

"Certainly! I love to regale an audience with a good tale of travel." Weathervane answers. "I would sell you one of our books, but sadly, they were in one of the bags we lost during the storm."

"Oh no! Did you lose a lot of items?" Briny asks, anxious that it may have been the storm whipped up on the mountain that caused the twins to lose their things.

"Not to worry. We lost some items, but most we can easily replace. I did lose my treasured moonstone necklace, and Compass lost a favorite tin and beautiful pen. Still, the items served us well while they were with us." Weathervane moves to fix the position of the basket's weights and check the straps.

Briny speaks up, confused, "Aren't you sad to have lost meaningful items? I don't understand why you aren't upset."

"Well sure," the explorer replies, "I'm a bit sad, but I know the necklace and other things will go on to help somebeing else. Over time, items get lost. Some things lose their usefulness to us, or are needed more by anotherbeing. That's one of the reasons we sometimes lose treasured items; they are needed elsewhere. I try to moderate my mourning over losing an item with good tidings for wherever the item is headed next." Smiling encouragement, Weathervane finishes checking the hot air balloon.

Tonic thinks about the beauty in this idea while fixing everyone some tea, and spends a moment being thankful to all the items lost over time, and all the ones found just when they are needed.

As the cups are passed around, Facet pipes up, "Why don't you and Compass travel together? Why one by air and one by land? Doesn't it sometimes get lonely being apart that way?"

Weathervane nods and replies, "For sure, it can get a bit lonesome. But we travel a similar path, and we meet up regularly to compare notes and swap stories. We get enough together time, we just like to travel different ways. I love flying, see; I always have! The skies, the wind and clouds, the treetops; ahhhh, a soothing balm for me. The ground makes me fidgety. It is too firm, too solid! I was hatched with wings that just don't fly, so when I was young I always felt nervous and unsettled. I was forever climbing higher and seeking out the air-currents of altitude! I wanted to fly and tried all sorts of schemes with kites and capes and deep breaths." The friends listen to Weathervane's story, enraptured. "My constant search for ways to fly were mirrored by Compass; mirrors are a bit in reverse, you know. While I wanted to touch the skies, Compass wanted to stay firmly on the ground; but since my twin's wings work, others were constantly urging poor Compass to 'fly like a proper bird.' Oh, Compass hated the prodding and teasing. What was wrong with just walking? We should all be allowed to move in ways that bring us joy. So while I was pitied for my ineffective wings, Compass was ridiculed for not using effective ones. We decided early on to find a job, a calling, that would allow us to work together, to help others, and to travel however we wanted! When we started our exploring endeavors, we both hiked, but I would always climb the tallest trees whenever we rested. Sometimes I would even travel the tree canopies while Compass walked below! Eventually, I discovered balloonships while in Gearlock, and now I'm hardly ever on the ground!"

A hearty cry of "Clear trails! How have you got it working, 'Vane?" rings out. Looking around, they spot a bird with a wide beak, walking across the meadow toward them, wearing a cable knit sweater and a sturdy backpack. "Ho! Fair winds, Compass! Some new friends helped me out!" Weathervane responds. The twins greet each other with compassion, and soon, all are being introduced and acquainted. Briny, Tonic, and Facet explain their journey, to which the twins are helpful and optimistic.

Compass assures the sprite, coblyn, and gnome that they are headed the correct direction. "I saw the depression full of violets when I was out gathering. I didn't go near it, but it shouldn't take you too much longer. The meadow itself is a lot of geography in a small space, very scrunched up, so it takes quite a while to cross. You are nearly out of it though, not to worry."

Tonic gives the Nightjar twins a tin of fruit blossom tea to enjoy on their travels. As the hot air balloon rises, Compass sets off walking again, wishing everyone, "Safe journeys, and may peace and joy be with you until we meet again!" When the balloon is high enough for a good view across the landscape, Weathervane points the trio toward the Tree Beyond the Garden.

"Well met, and meet again!" Tonic, Briny, and Facet all call as they head toward the Lintel.

Chapter 14: Lintel

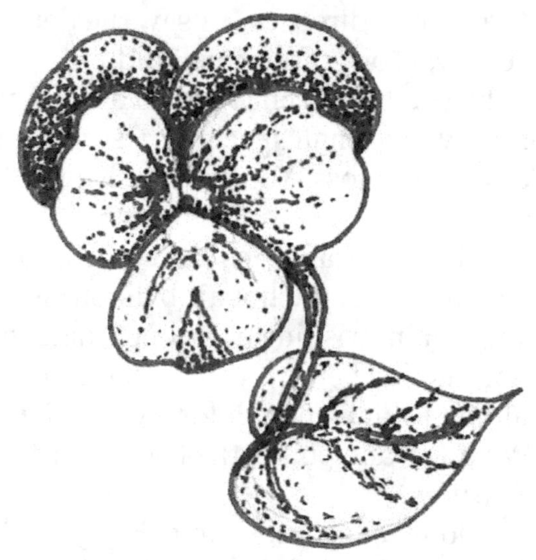

The walk across the rest of the meadow is gentle, and the time seems a good bit shorter than the first half was. While strolling along, Tonic abruptly swirls toward Facet and yelps, "Quick! Before they're gone!" while pointing at the hot air balloon floating slantwise to places unknown.

"What?!" The startled coblyn grinds to a halt and looks around with concern.

"The Useful Device! For seeing far away!" Tonic's bubbling enthusiasm makes it hard for the gnome to articulate thoughts clearly.

Briny gasps, "Oh! Yes, let's send the Nightjar twins your Useful Device! It would likely be so much help to them."

Tonic nods in grinning agreement.

"Of course! What a brilliant idea!" Facet responds with elation. Taking out the far-seeing Useful Device the coblyn wonders, "But how do we get it back to them? The meadow takes so long to cross."

"windrabbits," Briny asserts, while taking the Useful Device. With a sharp whistle, the sprite has all three windrabbits at attention. "It will take all of you working together, but please race this Useful Device up to the hot air balloon. Okay?" Spindrift twirls the Useful Device and takes the lead, showing Steam and Turbine how to lift and balance it. Facet writes a brief note of thanks and explanation, ripping the page out of the birchbark journal. Tonic uses a bit of ribbon from a tea tin to tie the note securely to the Useful Device. Only a few slips and drops later, the windrabbits are racing the Useful Device toward the ever more distant hot air balloon. Continuing their trek while the gift is delivered, the friends share the happy, satisfying feeling of helping.

The woods on the far side of the meadow loom up quite suddenly, as though the meadow was eager to have the trio arrive; or perhaps the geography is not as scrunched up at this end. Looking back across the meadow, Briny twists a rainbow bracelet and notices that the hot air balloon and the Nightjar twins are no longer visible. The sprite smiles, thinking of what Weathervane said about lost things, and quietly says, "It was magnificent to meet them. I hope they bring delight where they are needed next. Although the twins aren't exactly lost things, their friendship is treasured and I will miss them." Moments later, the speedy windrabbits are back.

Surveying the landscape ahead, the friends determine that the trees are large, the brambles tangled, and the undergrowth a thicket. It is hard work to get into the woods. Facet chooses a sharp Sudden Idea from the Birchbark journal to help cut into the brush. Tonic looks for a path with the least harmful plants, and uses the Mighty Teaspoon Hammer to sweep aside and tamp-down any flora blocking the way. Briny barrels through like a storm, ripping and stomping, and sometimes howling from a vicious thorn or stick. In this way, sprite, gnome, and coblyn make it through the dense outer layer of the woods.

Once inside, the light is a dappled green, and the air is cooler. The trees are older and larger, so the undergrowth is thinner, and making progress is much easier. The trio stops for a rest and a snack of nuts and dried fruit. The windrabbits chase up a breeze to cool everyone, and soon the friends are searching for the depression full of violets that marks the Tree Beyond the Garden. Facet uses the Sudden Idea about maps to help determine their course; the little Sudden Idea has pale, creamy wings with fine lines making a compass rose pattern in vibrant red, blue, yellow, and green on them. The underbrush has thickened again, and sturdy green vines curl and lock everything together, almost into a wall. Tonic observes, "Some of these vines are as thick as the bowl of my Mighty Teaspoon Hammer. We won't be able to cut them. But if Compass saw the hollow of violets, then there must be a way through. Look for any sort of break in the vines, or more cleared area."

The search is quite fruitless for a long while, until Facet notices the opening of a small tunnel in the thick greenery. "I'm not sure much more than a windrabbit could slip through there, though," the coblyn muses with disappointment.

"Not to worry!" Tonic exclaims, hauling the Mighty Teaspoon Hammer around. "It seems that most of the plants here are dead and brittle. I believe I can lever the tunnel open a bit bigger for us!" The gnome heaves and bashes with the Hammer, causing a crackling ruckus. Bits of vines and twigs clatter away as the tunnel widens. In a short time, bracken pieces fly and the air fills with viny bark dust. Clearing the debris, the trio sees that the tunnel is big enough to walk through in a crouch. The vines that are left are a vibrant green, and closely woven together, forming a tunnel that almost glows with verdant light.

Tonic goes through the vine tunnel first, to clear the way, Mighty Teaspoon Hammer held out and ready. Briny is next, gently herding the windrabbits. Since Facet is the tallest, the coblyn often bonks into a lower-hanging stick or bole, despite the crawling crouch they all use. The group is out of the tunnel faster than you can say "repeating regatta of revolving rafts is revolutionary!" Although why you should want to say that is unclear; it's not as though it pertains to the situation.

On the other side of the brief, leafy tunnel is a wide, grassy clearing; and a depression filled with violets! In the center is one twisted tree, on smooth, bare earth. The tree is smallish, possibly a peach tree, but totally barren. Not a leaf or flower on it. It is intriguing and enticing, though the trio could not explain why if anyone had asked. The party moves toward it, holding hands, unsure of what will happen. Tonic is on one end and slightly in the lead. "This is it," the gnome declares, "this is the Lintel. We've almost found Graemes!"

The moment Tonic's foot touches the cleared area, all three friends are filled with fear and a sense of dread and loss. Their hands clasp tighter, and none of them moves forward.

Chapter: 15
Notyet

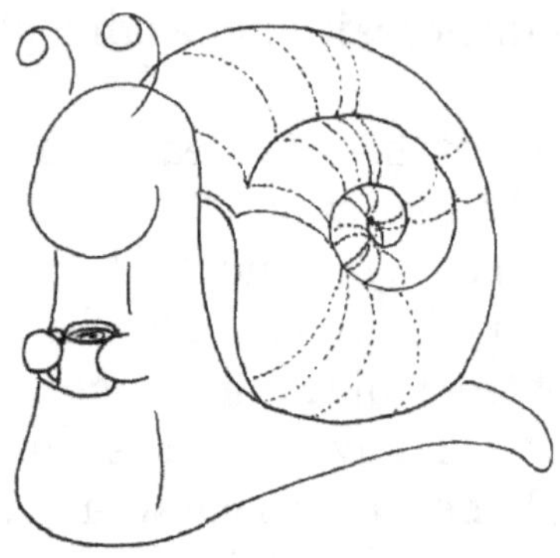

All three friends desperately want to run, but each stays on the circle of barren earth to help the other two; or possibly too scared to move themselves. Slowly, in this way, each individual only managing to stay in order to support their friends, the semi-paralyzed trio inches forward until gnome, sprite, and coblyn all stand completely on the desolate patch of ground. The reddish-grey dirt is dry and grainy; no interesting rocks beckon to Facet, no puddles call to Briny, no plants hope to sing with Tonic. The trio is held in place by fidgety anxiety, wriggling but not leaving. Then, with a very deep breath (one full of trepidation and uneasiness), Briny, Tonic, and Facet reach out to touch the Tree Beyond the Garden.

Facet waits anxiously; there is no mystical whooshing tunnel. Tonic tenses nervously; there are no sparkly lights opening a portal. Briny quickly loses patience and huffs in disappointment, "Wallowing currents! We've completed our Craft Conclusions, journeyed on a Wanderlust, met a dryad with a curse, were nearly stranded in a forest on our way to the Librarians, found a Knight and leveled a mountain, navigated an impossible village, crossed an endless meadow that's only 20 paces across, walked further than I've ever been from home... but we made it! We made it to this tree to find Graemes. And nothing happens?! What do we do now?"

Facet hesitates, "I...I don't know. I don't actually have a map with clearly labeled steps for how to complete this quest..."

Impacted by the friends' words, Tonic considers going home; there is no longer the pull of the Wanderlust, the adventure could be done, and they would surely meet Graemes whenever the mentor travels their way again. ...but that seems so unfulfilling. To have made it this far, past so much, only to be stopped at the last step? Yet the comforts of home beckon too.

Briny and Facet watch their friend thinking, waiting for some idea. The gnome pulls out Graemes' journal and reads the first decipherable portion to be found: "Whenever the world suddenly seems strange, when your heart races for no reason, when your senses sharpen and drink in every detail, when places you know are unfamiliar, when unknown places feel like home, that is a Lintel to the World's Between. Find the Lintel, and you can cross over. Although the Lintels and Marginalia are often extraordinary, the actual travel of the World's Between is gradual, often hardly noticed."

"That was surprisingly pertinent." Facet quips, trying to lighten the mood.

Looking around, searching for some indication of where to go or what to do, the trio remains baffled. They leave the circle around the dead tree and walk among the depression full of violets; the flowers are fragrant, the green of the vine tunnel is bright. Wandering back out of the vine tunnel,

Tonic wonders aloud, "Did we somehow miss the right tree? Is that one last piece of the Marginalia?; multiple trees in barren circles in depressions of violets, and we have to find the right one?"

When the trio is out of the tunnel again, Tonic turns in a confused circle. "Oh blister buds. Facet, can you tell from your Stratigraphy Skirt where we need to go? I can't figure it out."

As Facet begins pointing out subterranean features on the skirt, Briny notices a wiggly movement drop out of the birchbark journal and asks, "Facet; what's up with your birchbark?"

The three friends see the Sudden Idea about maps wriggle free of the journal and start hopping and spinning. "Maplet?" Facet asks, kneeling down close to the little Sudden Idea on the ground, "What do you want to tell me?" Maplet spins again, so it's rose-star wing-pattern twirls around, then points away into the thicket forest and squeaks at Facet. "Thank you, Maplet! Back into the birchbark now." Facet helps Maplet back into the bronze bag. "It seems we go this way," the coblyn indicates with a gesture the way the Sudden Idea is pointing. "Maplet is quite certain that although it isn't exactly the way we came, it's the way we need to go."

"Perhaps there *are* multiple trees, then, and we just chose the wrong one," Briny muses as the three friends start off again. The forest is as thick as before, full of brambles and untidy trees. Something seems different though, perhaps the lighting, or a scent in the air. All of the friends are quiet, as each tries to figure out what has changed, or if anything *has* changed. Tonic asks aloud, "*Is* anything different? Or did we just expect so hard for it to be, that now it seems slightly changed?"

The group continues on. Briny watches the sky as they walk, and eventually says to the friends, "It seems a good bit later in the day than it should be. Wasn't it still before lunch when we reached the tree? ...I think we are nearing late afternoon now."

Before any of them can think about this question, they come out in a large meadow of short grass, with a low, sprawling, brown box of a house in the center. There's a brightly painted wooden sign above the door that shows a snail in a ribbon-bow. The words above the image say The Snail's Gift in softly curved letters. Maplet lets out a contented trilling purr as the friends approach the building.

There is a friendly light glowing from the windows, a delicious smoky scent in the air, and a laughing bustle of activity from within. Tonic pulls open the door and follows Briny and Facet inside. The interior is all wood, with polished wood floors, scrubbed wood walls, and heavy wood beams that support the ceiling. There is a beautiful array of art displayed all over. The building has additions that ramble in different sizes, and slightly different heights from each other. The room they enter appears to be the main room, as it is a fairly large cube, seating roughly 8 full tables of guests, plus some smaller tables of guests besides. There is an open archway on the far wall, and a small step up, leading to the next room.

Entering this second room, the friends see that it is about the same size and shape as the first, with windows looking out the back meadow, and more travelers eating and talking. There is a kitchen built on from the second room, the grain and color of the wood (and another, differently-sized step down) suggesting it is a further addition. To the left and right, the main length of the building, there are some hallways that appear to lead off to other rooms (probably bedrooms for rent). The atmosphere is warm and welcoming, with a fair number of beings seated all around, and eating an evening meal. Briny, Facet, and Tonic are greeted by somebeing carrying a tray of fresh fruit bowls. The friends can see a kind face peeking from behind the tray.

"Hello, and how's the road? I haven't seen you in the Snail's Gift before. I'm Notyet the Snail, owner. You seem a bit bewildered; would you like a meal?" Wearing a sturdy yellow apron, patient expression, rounded glasses framing dark green eyes, and hair pulled up into a dark brown, teal, and white swirling bun, the innkeeper waits expectantly for a reply.

Tonic's tummy wombles loudy, and they all agree that they are hungry. Notyet guides them to a table and gives them fresh fruit, warm pumpkin-sage soup, and lavender lemonade."It's the last of the batch, so just a few Beans for it." Not yet says. Coblyn, sprite, and gnome happily pay the meagre price and eat gratefully at first, but soon slow down. The food is delicious, but they still feel uneasy because their heads are full of worries about their journey; this doesn't appear to be the World of Myth, they don't know how to cross the Lintel of the Tree Beyond the Garden, and they have no idea what to do to find Graemes now.

After a while of cooking, bringing meals, clearing dishes, and tending the kitchen, Notyet notices the new guests looking despondent, their food only half-nibbled. The snail goes to the trio's table, hoping to help them.

"What brings you here? I've been running this inn for a long time. Can I help you find anything?" Notyet offers.

Briny fusses, "We were on a Wanderlust, but we seem to be stuck. We've been through so much and gotten to the Tree Beyond the Garden, but we can't figure out how to cross the Lintel, which means we have no idea how to find Graemes."

Notyet nods sympathetically. "That does sound troublesome. Can you tell me more of your journey?"

Facet adds in more details of their travel. Tonic describes Graemes, and how the Wanderlust and everything started. Briny cuts in with clarifications. Soon, the friends have eaten their meal and told their whole story.

Notyet exclaims, "Quite the coddiwomple!... You've had

such a purposeful journey, but to a rather vague destination. I think I can help, though. You did cross the Lintel, you are in the World of Myth. Well, nearly in the World of Myth. I keep my Snail's Gift right on the edge. The worlds fade a bit into each other, so you don't always notice right away. And there's always a change from traveling the World's Between. You should notice it soon enough. Don't be too surprised if the changes seem like a steep price for traveling the World's Between. It's different for everyone, so I don't know what to tell you to expect. I recommend resting up, then heading out in the morning. When you go, you'll want to follow the paved path; paving is like smooth stone. I'll show you after breakfast."

The three friends are frozen in fascination. "We DID cross?" Tonic asks with confusion.

"How would we even know?!" Briny pipes up, with an anxious twirl of a bracelet; "There was no real change! We could have just wandered around lost forever!"

Facet yawns wide, thinking about the ancient myths, "I think maybe that explains a lot. The old myths and stories about not leaving the path, about fantastical characters suddenly showing up and disappearing... it rather makes sense that travelers often didn't even realize when or how they crossed the World's Between." Briny, Tonic, and Facet ponder this idea for a moment. Then with tired stretches and full tummies, the friends thank Notyet and pay for the accommodation. The snail shows them to a comfy room, then hurries off to finish cleaning the kitchen. Tonic comments sleepily "I'm exhausted, like all the hours we lost are catching up."

Chapter 16: Wildlings

After a restful night at the Snail's Gift, Tonic, Facet, and Briny are excited to be on their way. Facet does a quick count, and realizes their coins are getting low; they will need to be thrifty. Finding Graemes and their journey's end seem very close, and they are once again full of fizzy energy. The windrabbits remain asleep in their bag, satchel, and pouch, as coblyn, sprite, and gnome go to break their daily fast in the main room of the inn.

Notyet is busy cooking, cleaning, and generally tending to the inn and various guests while the trio enjoy a hot cereal of oats, buckwheat, and hemp seeds, with maple cream, chopped pecans, and fresh huckleberries on top. As the friends are finishing their meal, Notyet's work slows down, and the snail comes over to chat, "You seem to have learned a good bit about the World's Between from your friend Graemes. I will try to help fill in any gaps in your knowledge before you go. Do you have questions?"

"Yes," Facet is ready to take notes. "Can anybeing travel the Worlds Between? I understand the Lintels and Marginalia keep accidental crossing to a minimum, but are there people who cannot go? Could a group like us be separated, if not everyone is a Wildling? Are there limits to how much we travel?"

Notyet nods, "You have many good questions. As you've said, a Wildling is one who can travel the World's Between. The word for someone who cannot sense or travel the World's Between is 'Glazed.' The Glazed cannot sense a Lintel, they do not get the "wild" feeling a Wildling has. When a Lintel is near, Wildlings describe an experience of the world shifting, of feeling newness, or magic, or of the world seeming brighter or more urgent. So no, not everyone travels the World's Between." Notyet looks at the group and continues, "As for a group traveling together, it may be possible for a Glazed to travel the World's Between with the help of a Wildling, but I do not know. I'm not sure it's ever been tested scientifically. Most beings regard the World's Between as made-up, magic, fantasy, mere legend; those few who do travel are usually too busy traveling and having adventures to test the science of it." Here the snail hurries off to clear away the dirty dishes.

With a hand-flutter Facet looks at Briny and Tonic, "We were doing so much, I never really considered... are we really going into the World of Myth? Where tricksy humans trap us and steal our science and skills? Where we get turned to stone? It hardly seems like something real..."

Briny's changeable moods flow between surprise, disbelief, and anger, settling near confusion. "I never really thought...Not real? I mean, Graemes *does* travel, Graemes goes *somewhere*. And the journal mentions the World's Between. And Nightshade said the World of Myth is real, and Vellum agreed; Notyet too. I mean, how would it even be some elaborate prank?"

Tonic pats the pocket with the plush moth in it, "I'm sure the World of Myth is real, but... well, just like any story, maybe bits of it are made up? Maybe it's really just another part of the real world? I just don't think magic can really be real."

Notyet returns from cleaning and continues, "Your last question is about limits on travel; again, not much rigorous scientific testing has been done about traveling the World's Between. There aren't as many Wildlings as there once were; however, I do get a fair amount of travelers, and they all have stories. While I've never heard of strict limits, travelers do report changes. Some changes might cause you to choose to limit your travels across the World's Between. Do you know what happens when you finish crossing the Lintel? Rules between worlds don't always match. What works on one side may be different on the other. The reward of growth requires risk; some beings who travel the World's Between change but little, some change a lot. I have heard of some for whom time passes differently between worlds, and some whose body shape changes, some find they speak differently, some lose abilities or knowledge. Travel together, stay kind and adaptable, and you should fare pretty well." The snail offers a cloth package to the trio, "Here, it's your first trip. Take some apples and bread. The World of Myth is strange, and it's always helpful to have at least one meal on you. Do you have anything you want me to send back home for you?" The trio shake their heads. "No? Okay. Now, follow me." Before any of the friends can say thanks, Notyet opens a door down the hall and points outside with a rainbow umbrella. "The smooth grey path there. That's a paved road. Seamint I think it's called. It will take you the rest of the way to the World of Myth."

Giving profuse thanks to Notyet, gnome, coblyn, and sprite head down the paved path of Seamint.

After a while, "This path has nothing to do with the sea."

Briny notes.

With a small sneeze, Tonic agrees, "Nor has it anything to do with mint!"

Facet takes a small piece of the smooth grey path to examine more closely, when Briny lets out a gasp. Facet wants to check on the sprite, but feels it is important to study this bit of stone from the path first. Looking at the grain and texture, Facet is certain they could understand the place they were going better, if the stone would just make sense; The geography feels all wrong, and Facet's muscles itch. The coblyn lowers the smoked goggles to help block out the glaring light.

Tonic rushes over to help Briny, who has fallen to the ground. "Are you okay? What happened?!"

Briny looks grumpy and bewildered. "My legs just stopped working! I didn't feel a sting, or a rock turn under me or anything! I just can't seem to get up."

Tonic nods and tries to comfort Briny, "Here, use the Mighty Teaspoon Hammer to support yourself." The gnome slings the Mighty Teaspoon Hammer around and pulls off the strap, offering it to Briny. The sprite tries to use it for balance, but quickly discovers its shape and weight make the Mighty Teaspoon Hammer an imperfect tool for this particular job. Tonic's concern grows, "Let me see what I can find to help out. There might be some branches for crutches or a plant to help with healing. Do you see any comfrey plants? They have fuzzy stems, and purple flowers."

Looking around for some way to help, Tonic sees a metallic-looking cylinder just ahead on the path. The top and bottom are silver, but the main portion is red, with white writing. Tonic goes and picks it up with curiosity; it fits easily in a hand and is a perfect cylinder, with top and bottom closed, but it feels petal-light. Deciding to take the metal thing to Facet, Tonic looks further up, and sees the circle of house bones.

Chapter 17: Mythwold

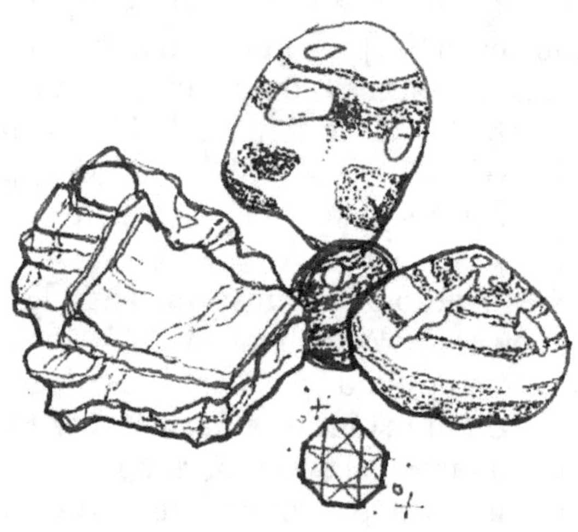

Back up the trail on the Seamint path, Facet slowly moves over to sit by Briny, collecting rocks along the way. Neither friend speaks.

The sprite is vexed and resentful, trying to stand, prodding indignantly at the useless legs, wishing the Mighty Teaspoon Hammer could fix things, and silently attempting to figure out what's going on; this world is an amazing bustle of unusual plants and animals, with fresh sky colors, and new scents in the air! Briny grumbles with frustration at being thwarted in exploring all this inspiring newness. The sprite of storms and seas takes several deep breaths, marveling at the unusual breezes: there are floral and grassy smells, surprising oily and smokey scents, and a faint waft of something sweet and savory. The wind and water here are full of all new stories!

Facet is feeling overwhelmed by the over-bright lights,

sharp scents, and incessant noises. To calm down, the coblyn starts sorting the new rock collection, noting their colors, textures, and sizes, organizing and reorganizing them in different patterns. First the large orange one, then the smooth striped one, next the greenish bumpy one, and the curiously translucent angular one, finally the small sparkly one on the miniature silver post. The coblyn keeps trying to tell Briny that everything will be okay, that the rocks just need to be in the right order for it all to work out, but for some reason Facet can't seem to communicate ideas very well. The buzz of unfamiliar insects, and the roar of distant beasts is very distracting, not to mention the continued itching, twitching sense of unease that keeps breaking Facet's concentration. Facet brushes the rounded edges of the goggles; the cool metals and soft furs make a good pattern. The coblyn's inspiring demeanor isn't functioning like usual; the world is loud and strange and prickly, but these stones are soothing. Facet admires the rocks, rolling their textures around in cupped hands, always rotating the stones in patterns of five. The world is too much of everything right now; feelings of fear, disappointment, and anger all squeeze together inside Facet, unable to get out, and building pressure. The coblyn's hands flutter.

Briny looks over at the constant scraping-clunking noise Facet is making with the tumbling rocks, and groans. "Salty bladderwrack, Facet! What has happened to you?" glaring in alarm at the coblyn's physical changes, like hair and skin colors and textures, the sprite flips frothy curls. Knowing the sensation isn't right, Briny turns with trepidation toward a reflective puddle to gawk at what their own changes might be.

Staring at the stark scene of construction, Tonic notices how the grey Seamint path curves most of the way around the circle. There are five box-houses, their partially-built bones tall and stark. Each box-house has a tiny, short-grass meadow around it. The house bones sit just outside the grey path; in the center of the Seamint circle is a smooth, black surface that looks almost sticky (but is firm and dry to Tonic's cautious touch). A movement catches the gnome's attention, and Tonic braces for an attack before realizing it's just a reflection in the window of the nearest partial-house.

Looking closer at the reflection, it is apparent that the green is missing from Tonic's hair puffs; they are a solid shade of dark walnut brown; well, not solid brown; there are lighter tans and whites where the gnome's leaves and mosses used to be. With a soft, bewildered touch to a hair puff, Tonic notes other changes: "My eyes still have warm orange flecks, but why are they mostly brown now?" The gnome's moss and lichen patches and bark-like skin are altered too; the lichens and mosses are missing, leaving instead pale patterns on the delicate, smooth brown skin. "Where has my tough bark gone? Where are my lichens?" Tonic wonders aloud. Marveling and still gripping the perfect, red metal cylinder, Tonic lets out a loud yelp when a voice nearby says, "Are you going to drink that soda?"

Chapter 18:
Soda

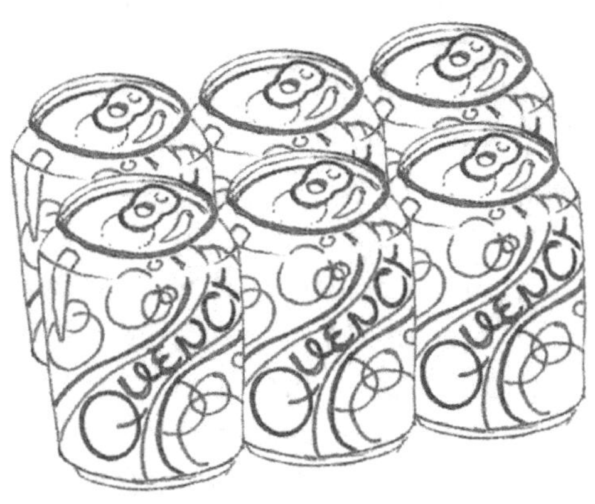

After the brief scream of surprise, Tonic stammers "W-what? Who..?" The gnome's wide eyes take in a figure in odd, fantasy clothes, with pictures of crafts drawn on their arms, wavy dyed-green-and-blue hair in a low ponytail, and sturdy, dark boots on their feet. "From your expressions and clothing, I'm guessing you came from Fierlund. Here they call it Fairyland or the Land of Legend. I'm Petrichor - I'm a tylwyth teg. Don't worry; this building site is deserted, there is nothing here to hurt you. Most paths from Myth to Legend come out somewhere abandoned. I'm not sure why, though. Maybe it's easier to build a path where it won't run into stuff? I like to walk through and admire the quiet; it's a melancholy sort of beauty here. Anyways, hello! How can I help?"

With another sneeze and a snuffle, Tonic looks again at the metal cylinder. The gnome's mind is in a whirl trying to figure out what to ask, or say, or do. "I don't... What's a 'soh-da'? And can you please help? My friend's legs aren't working," is the best the gnome can manage.

Petrichor pipes up, "Let's go look; I'll do my best to help. Is this your first time traveling to the World of Myth?" Tonic nods as they walk back to Briny, and the tylwyth teg continues, "Ah. Well, then. Have you discovered how you've changed yet? I lost my ability with plants; I can't grow anything anymore. I create gardens in paper and paint now. I've learned ever so much, but it is a blow to lose my connection with living plants; I don't even change with the seasons anymore, and as you can see my hair is no longer plants."

Tonic realizes that Petrichor's whole outfit is adorned with plant imagery; buttons that look like flowers, embroidered patches of leaves and blooms, a hair tie knitted to look like a vine, even plant patterns woven into the cloth. The gnome says with honesty, "I'm so sorry; that sounds really difficult. I can't imagine not being able to interact with plants!" Tonic rubs a pale arm-patch while remembering the tea garden at home, and misses the familiar sights, sounds, and smells.

Ahead of them are the figures of Facet and Briny. Tonic gestures to the two friends, asking Petrichor, "Can you help Briny?" Tonic remembers the earlier reflection and all the changes it showed, and uneasily tries to take in Facet and Briny's changes: Facet's hair no longer looks like lustrous quartz and hidden gems, but more like pale straw, with skin less like marbled ochre and kaolin clays, and instead a simple, muted tawny brown. The coblyn seems introspective, not vocal and full of ideas. Briny's hair is no longer splashing ocean waves, but is stationary and curled, pale brown in color; and the sprite's skin is bland and peach-ish like a newt, instead of the angry ripples of tidal pools and riverstones; at least Briny's eyes are still mer-grotto blue. Tonic is taken aback to see how the three of them seem to have lost all of their unique distinction, and for a moment the gnome can't tell them apart.

Tonic's muddled reverie is broken as Petrichor offers, "I don't know if I can help, but I can do basic first aid." Petrichor plops a rucksack on the ground and rummages through while muttering "Wallet, hair tie, chap stick, old receipts... Hah! First aid kit." The tylwyth teg opens the little box first aid kit and looks over the disgruntled Briny's legs after taking the sprite's temperature. After some careful bends and observations of Briny's limbs Petrichor says, "So there's no pain in your legs? No feeling? I'm no professional healer, but nothing looks especially bruised or broken. If you could walk fine a minute ago, then... well, then perhaps this is your price for crossing the World's Between. Some of the myths say travelers might have to give up their name, or years of time in a few minutes, or the color of their eyes; my theory is that you don't actually lose what color your iris appears to be, but rather the ability to see color. Losing your legs certainly seems along those lines." Briny gives a surly frown, while tugging at a curl of hair, and Petrichor continues, "My house isn't far; I live in the apartments on the other side of that fence. Would you all like a snack? We can take turns helping Briny over to my house." Looking over the fence, Tonic and Briny notice a lot of bustle and noise. Petrichor continues, "Our apartment complex put on a food festival today, so everyone is about, checking out the snacks and getting balloons and face-paint. We can get some good food from there, once we have Briny sorted."

Happy for guidance and for the energy of a community, Tonic says, "Thank you; that sounds great. I'm Tonic, by the way. Briny, Facet, what do you think?"

Briny looks up dolefully from the ground, "Well, I need *some* way to get around. I don't think I can crawl everywhere. Have you seen these new plants?! And the skyscape is unreal! Honestly, I really thought that once we got to the World of Myth, everything would be wonderful, Graemes would magically be right here, and we could have some amazing experience, and then we would all go home. It seems like there is always one more step. Now that I'm here, this place is *astonishing*, but there is no Graemes here, and I can't even explore any of it!" The sprite nearly whines the last bit, admitting a hard truth.

"Yes," Petrichor nods solemnly, "Some tasks are like that. I find it best every day to just keep trying to do the next right thing. Here, Briny, climb on my back and I'll carry you."

Tonic picks up the Mighty Teaspoon Hammer and rucksack as they start to follow the tylwyth teg, then looks around and asks, "Facet? Are you coming? Is everything okay?" The coblyn remains paused on the Seamint path, looking at the ground.

Facet's hushed answer comes after a momentary pause, "Yes. Facet, are you coming? Yes." then the gnome's voice gets stronger, "Did you know most rocks are just a type of quartz? And calling a stone 'jasper' sounds fancy, but it's almost as vague as saying 'quartz.'" Facet quietly picks up the collection of rocks, rearranging them in one hand. "...Three, four, five..." The rocks stop, and start tumbling the other direction in the gnome's hand. Facet's thoughts zip and fizzle, jumping from rocks here, to stones at home, to the sheen on polished metal, the shape of Tonic's windows, the Clickfish basin, an axle Clover recently broke and a solution on how to fix it, the smoothest stone being held, the color and flavor of really good pie, warm days picking fresh berries, the 14 distinct colors of rocks on the path so far...

"No, I didn't know that, Facet. Are you okay?" Tonic asks. Facet nods, and keeps twiddling the rocks and touching the patterns of smooth metal and soft furs on the goggles, while following Tonic using peripheral vision (Facet's thoughts keep jumping, "Are the metals here the same? My shoes are too tight. I could use another pocket. I need to keep a stone in my pocket, what do a bird's feathers feel like, could the clouds move differently here, I'm thirsty, how is no one else upset by all the **noise**?...). Facet's thoughts churn at lightning speed, but communication with others is slow and difficult. The rocks flash, roll, and rotate in the coblyn's hand: orange, striped, greenish, clear, sparkly; then smallest to largest, then bumpy, smooth, oval, sharp, flaky, and on and around the rocks go. Facet feels safer behind the goggles in this loud, distracting place.

Tonic looks with apprehension at Briny and Facet, and worries about their unusual changes.

Petrichor carries Briny most of the way to the apartment complex, and Tonic carries the rucksack. The group hurries through the crowd of festival-goers, ogling the tents and metal caravans and unusual treats. The sprite is especially struck by the wonder of the unfamiliar creatures and things; hardly any forest, no ocean, hot black paths, smooth, squared buildings, and cracking energy zipping invisibly everywhere (like a storm that decided it doesn't need clouds). With wide blue-grey eyes, Briny tries to understand all the flashing, glittering sights.

They approach a large, bland building, and Petrichor heads for a white, rectangular door that has a colorful woven vine wreath adorning it. The wreath adds individuality with its bright purples, greens, and oranges from the flowers woven into it. Most of the other doors and walls look all the same: dull, muted colors, and all the same shape, size, and spacing. Inside, Petrichor's first floor apartment is small and moderately tidy, adorned with paintings of plants, fiber flowers in vases, and various blooms and leaves. Putting Briny on the couch, Petrichor laughs and points, asking, "Tonic, *do* you intend to drink that soda? If you want to save it for later, we can put it in the fridge."

"Oh!" The gnome is surprised to see the red metal cylinder still in one hand. "What is it? I found it on the ground and was going to ask Facet about it. Facet is great with stones and metals."

"It's a soda. A sort of sweet, bubbly drink." Petrichor explains. "It's put into the can to keep it fresh and makes it easy to travel with. Here, let me show you how they work." Tonic hands over the can and the tylwyth teg remarks with confusion, "Wow! That's light; it feels empty." Petrichor shakes the can with a concerned frown, looking it over as Tonic and Briny watch. Facet sits on the floor, rolling a stone in one hand. Petrichor observes, "No holes or punctures anywhere, but I don't hear a slosh either," then pries at the small metal tab to break open the sealed hole in the can. The can is completely empty.

Chapter 19: Petrichor

Petrichor is momentarily awed by the unexpectedly empty can, then the tylwyth teg laughs, saying, "Well, that's bizarre! But I guess there are always a few odd things where worlds meet. I have a few sodas left over from when Wynn last visited. You can try one of those, if you want." Pertrichor goes to a large metal rectangle, and opens the front, releasing a cool rush of air. "I hate for you not to be able to try soda after all that build-up!"

Pulling out another metal cylinder like the empty one Tonic had, Petrichor opens it with a click and a foaming-hissing noise. Tonic jumps back, moving to protect Briny and Facet; despite the loud crack and commotion, nothing harmful seems to happen. Petrichor pours the soda into 4 cups, taking a sip first, then offering it around. "Be careful, it is very fizzy at first!" the tylwyth teg cautions brightly. Briny flips and twirls a curl of hair while cautiously accepting the proffered drink.

With a few sips and sputters, and a bubbly burp through the nose, Tonic and Briny decide this drink is to be sipped sparingly. The two cups are put down carefully, but firmly, as though they are slightly dangerous. Considering the fizzy, prickly burp Briny's nose had, perhaps they ARE a bit dangerous. Facet looks at the drink placed on a nearby coaster, then continues to work with the stones, sorting by number of divots, then by best texture for smoothing a pinkie against.

After putting away the extra soda, Petrichor looks pensive. "How do we get you mobile, Briny? I don't have a wheelchair handy. Can you stand at all? I think I still have my crutches and leg brace. Ideally, You should go to a doctor to see exactly what is wrong and probably do physical therapy to regain mobility, but without any money or ID, that will be difficult. I think a short-term solution will have to do for now."

Briny agrees, "I really want to be able to finish our quest, and I don't think I can do that by staying in one spot." With a wry smirk the sprite adds, "And I really don't fancy crawling everywhere, when there is so much to experience!"

While the tylwyth teg is looking further into the house for the promised crutches and brace, Tonic decides to check in with Facet, who has been so quiet here in Mythwold. Facet still sits on the floor, admiring a hand-sized tree sculpture made of twisted wire, with small gems for leaves, which sits on a low table. "What did you find, Facet?" Tonic asks, and continues after a pause: "How are you feeling about all of this? You've been unusually quiet." Facet takes some time answering, while fidgeting and looking uncomfortable. Then with hands fluttering the coblyn blurts out in a rush, "The rocks here are stunning! Could I take home all the rocks and wire? I want to put them in the right order at home. This wire is coated with silver, but has a copper or nickel base. Have you looked at the rocks? The smooth one is best for my pinkie, but in my palm I like the bumpy one. I have 17 kinds of Jasper at home. This is a new quartzite, and this may well be serpentine." Puzzled, Tonic wonders if the World's Between took something of Facet's ability to communicate, or to focus on anything besides rocks.

Just then the friends hear a loud "Ah-HAH!" from the other room. Briny frowns doubtfully when Petrichor returns with some sticks and cloth. "Those don't exactly look like a cure..." Briny says with concern while twisting a rainbow bracelet.

"Well, no," Petrichor confirms, "but if you can use your legs some, these will help do the extra work. See, you put the padded part of the crutches under your arms so they can bear your weight, then you can use them a bit like legs as you swing yourself forward." Petrichor demonstrates the process. "And this is a leg brace; it helps steady and secure your knee. Will you try them? Then we can go out to the apartment's mini festival, and see about introducing you to the world a little more." A sloshing gurgle interrupts them, causing Petrichor to add, "and get some snacks for hungry tummies!"

After a few failed attempts full of struggle and frustration, Briny plops onto the couch, saying, "This is exhausting!" During all this, Facet has been wandering quietly around the room, preoccupied, and gently touching every surface.

Tonic is tired and vexed at seeing Facet and Briny unwell and struggling. "Why isn't this working?!" the gnome snaps. "This whole world is magic! It's Mythwold! Literally the World of Myth! All of our amazing stories and myths come from here! You have captured the frozen winter wind to keep food and houses cool, and caged lightning in little globes to create the day whenever you want, you have spells to move metal restaurants around, and sharp, tickling bubbles trapped in your drinks! This place oozes magic, but we still can't find Graemes, and now Briny and Facet are missing parts of themselves!" Tonic gestures emphatically.

"It's not all magic, you know," Petrichor cuts in. "It's all science, just like at home. What is magic anyway? It seems like each world has rules to follow, and understanding those rules is called science. It's just different science than ours." Sighing, the tylwyth teg straps some thick padded bandages around Briny's knees and continues, "I'm sorry, I wish I had a magic, instant cure. But if Briny is able to use these crutches and knee braces, they will help your mobility a lot! I'll call up Wynn. She can help; she's an EMT."

Tonic and Briny stare at Petrichor in confusion. Briny asks, "...What is "she"? What does that mean?" while Tonic asks, "Is an Ee Ehm Tea a kind of herbal wizard?"

Before Petrichor can answer any questions, Facet stops rummaging through the bronze bag and suddenly speaks up, with a quiet, but forceful question, "Why can't I see Turbine? Where are the windrabbits?" The coblyn's brown eyes are wide with worry.

Briny gives an unconcerned laugh, "You know them. They are around. They love playing Gusty Spin. I am sure they will be back messing up our papers and knocking things over soon. Maybe when they come back they can help bolster me along."

Tonic nods and smiles at Briny, knowing how much their windrabbits love to play and roam. Facet continues to search, looking behind curtains, under chairs, on top of books, and in every improbable place around the room. The gnome's hands flutter to help reduce the thoughts rushing around.

Chapter 20: Winn

"It's pretty anticlimactic to come all the way to the World of Myth just to sit in my apartment." Petrichor says, "Let's take a tour and get to the apartment complex's festival to have snacks! And that means," the tylwyth teg continues with a smile at Briny, "getting you mobile! I've called Wynn and she should be by soon."

"Right!" Briny looks at Petrichor with interest. "You said that word before, 'she.' What does that mean?"

Facet goes digging through the bronze bag again, and finds the small, stripy birchbark journal. The coblyn sits down and opens it, trying to catch some of the spinning thoughts and ideas on the page.

Petrichor's lips twist while the tylwyth teg considers how to explain. "Well, this took some time for me to understand. In Fierlund, we are all different types of creatures and we generally put a lot of importance on our creature type or our job when referring to someone. Like, I might call Facet a coblyn, or I might say 'Steeper' instead of using Tonic's name. Here in Mythwold it doesn't work that way. People often use pronouns like "he" or "she" which references, apparently, their job in creating new beings. Here people require two creatures to create new beings; males use 'he/his' pronouns and females use 'she/her.' But this binary view isn't really true to what exists and how people feel, so some people started to use alternate pronouns like 'they/them'. Some bodies may be built one way, but the person feels differently."

Facet continues to look at the book, doodling in the edges of some pages. Briny looks dubious at the tylwyth teg's explanation, so Petrichor continues trying to explain, "Tonic you said you are a Steeper, right? And you *know* you love tea, correct? And Briny, you said you love the ocean. So what if our culture defined beings as either tea-loving or ocean-loving, and linked this to physical characteristics? Maybe it was believed and taught that tea-lovers have two arms and two lungs. Tonic has those, and Tonic loves tea, so Tonic matches that category; great! But what if we also defined ocean-lovers as having no arms, and gills to breathe water? Briny doesn't have either. Briny *looks* like a tea-lover, but Briny *knows* in their core that they are an ocean-lover! It would be very uncomfortable for Briny to live looking a different way than they feel. That's why I try to ask how I should refer to people; and I keep to the traditions of Fierlund by using they/them, a name, or job title if I'm not sure about the pronouns; I don't want to make people uncomfortable."

Tonic and Briny think this over while Petrichor tries to round out the explanation, "And of course, some beings like *both* tea *and* the ocean. Some enjoy neither. And somebeings like tea on cold days, but the ocean on hot ones, or mostly like tea, but sort of like the ocean, or any number of other combinations!" Petrichor takes a breath and wraps up, "I have heard that some languages here already use generic pronouns that simply mean 'a person' without defining their maleness or femaleness. Here where I am, though, the use of 'they/them' is resisted by some people because they insist that 'they/them' means a group, a plural of people, rather than just one singular person. As a society, the people here also default to 'he' if they don't know whether the person is male or female." after a brief pause, Petrichor finishes up, "It's A LOT to understand."

"That seems unfair!" Tonic pipes up with a furrowed brow. "I would hate to be constantly called a Storm Chaser if I was really a Steeper. So are there more male things than female? Is that why they guess 'he' if they don't know? Because it's more likely to be correct?"

Petrichor lets out a small sigh, "Nope. This whole thing took me *ages* to understand, and I still don't really get why they do what they do. There are about equal males and females, and some beings don't feel they fit fully in either category, or like they fit in both. The he/she binary, and default to 'he' just doesn't reflect their reality, even though it is still the way this culture is structured. There are a lot of rules and things to understand; don't fret too much about it, but do realize it's different than what you are used to."

"Rude." Briny grumbles, thinking about how it would feel if beings insisted on defining jobs without knowing, or refused to be corrected.

"Honestly," Petrichor agrees, "it has led to a lot of unnoticed and ingrained inequality in their society."

Facet moves the small collection of rocks around in different orders, counting, "16, 17, 18, 19, 20..." and draws the stones in all angles and configurations on some blank pages of the journal.

"So this Ee Ehm Tea you mentioned is a she?" Tonic asks. Petrichor nods. "So what are we?" the gnome wonders. "How do you tell 'she' from 'he'?"

Petrichor lets out a whistling sigh, "Ohhhh, that's difficult.

Like I said, I usually say 'they,' or use their name, or a description, until the person tells me. I'm really not good at judging or understanding the nuances of 'she' versus 'he.' A lot of people here say females are quiet and demure, kind, nurturing, clean, home caretakers; that males are loud and mean, rough, dirty, strong, outdoorsy leaders. But I have found this to be *completely* untrue. I think it is one of those ingrained beliefs that just doesn't match reality. I was really confused about all sorts of things when I first arrived here. Even though Wynn helped me a lot, I still needed someone else to help me sort out all my feelings. Wynn was great, and found a therapist for me to go to. Discussing my situation, my anger and confusion, really helped. It is a big change to move, especially so unexpectedly, and so much of the culture and social rules are so different! I loved having a safe space, and a person to talk to who is trained to help."

On the floor, Facet flips quickly through the book, searching for something, and thoughts tumbling like pebbles in a landslide "The windrabbits are still missing, Tonic seems to be agitated, how will we get home, Briny wants to go explore but is having trouble walking, do I have any Bits or Pieces left, noodles would be good right now..."

"Why did you come here to Mythwold?" Briny asks.

"And why haven't you gone back to Fierlund?" Tonic wonders with a worried frown.

"I came here by accident." Petrichor explains. "I was living happily in Fierlund, tending plants, helping with Growing Season. One day I had this terrible longing for a place. I don't know what place, it was just a strong, wistful urge to be... somewhere. Like homesickness, but not for any home I've ever known. I suppose it was a type of Wanderlust. I decided to take a break from the Growing, and travel for a bit. I ended up passing by this inn called The Snail's Gift one day, and as I turned the corner I ended up here. There was more construction going on then, as they were still trying to do a little building here, but most of the activity was building this apartment complex. I was so scared and confused I ended up running into one of the construction vehicles and getting a mild concussion. Wynn was the EMT who responded to the worker's call for help. I'm so thankful she was there to help me. I took a lot of helping, and over time we became great friends! I find the world here confusing, but fascinating, too; like the joyful brain-tickle of working out a puzzle, or learning a new skill. It is fun, but really, I stayed here in the World of Myth largely because of Wynn. She helped me feel comfortable here, and I do love exploring this world; it has a plethora of fascinating inventions! And some baffling ideas too."

There is knocking at the white door to the outside, which opens to reveal a figure taller than Petrichor, long creamy-yellow hair pulled back in a braid, wearing sturdy boots, long pants, and a short sleeved button-up shirt covered in bright patterns. "Hello, house!" the cheerful voice calls.

Petrichor smiles with delight. "Wynn! Welcome. This is why I called you." The tylwyth teg gestures to the sprite sitting on the couch. "Briny's legs stopped working suddenly. We've tried out my old crutches and leg brace, but I think you would do a better job of helping than I am."

"How is the festival?" Wynn asks, walking over to inspect Briny's legs. The sprite snorts in frustration, wanting to be up and moving already.

"It seems to be a success," Petrichor responds, "but we only saw it briefly as we hurried in to help Briny. I really want to get Briny, Facet, and Tonic out to experience it; I think they would enjoy it," the tylwyth teg explains while motioning to each of the friends.

Wynn works with Briny, coaching and encouraging to get the sprite moving again. Tonic and Petrichor cheer and assist as needed. After some practice, Briny is able to amble around a bit using the crutches. Wynn expresses joy at Briny's success, then says, "Your gait is still a bit awkward, as though your muscles had atrophied, or," Wynn examines Briny's legs again, "even twisted to work differently. You don't seem actively wounded in any way. I don't mean to pry, but do you have a longer history of walking difficulties? Your muscles move like you aren't used to these legs."

Briny grumbles a frustrated reply, "I'm used to being a lot more fluid. This is the first time this has happened."

Wynn gives a small nod, "You don't owe me an explanation. I just wondered if there was more I could do to help. I think you should be able to get around by using the crutches, if you are careful.""

Chapter 21: Festival

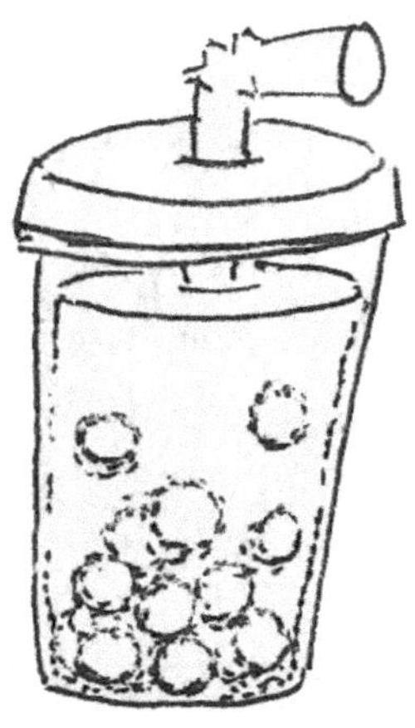

The group (consisting of Petrichor, Tonic, Facet, Wynn, and Briny) all head outside to the apartment's mini festival. Wynn insists that Briny leads; "A group should follow the pace of the slowest mover, so that no one gets left behind. This way, Briny can feel at ease and be able to practice getting around with the crutches, and we will all be able to enjoy the festival." So Briny leads, with Wynn nearby to assist, and Petrichor chats, while Tonic keeps an eye on Facet (who follows along behind, petting a small mottled stone, and looking through the birchbark journal). The hubbub dazzles the friends; Facet adjusts the goggles more snugly and hunches down.

Tonic is in awe of all the amazing sights, sounds, and smells, then sneezes a small puff of yellow pollen. "It's like a festival back home! (achoo) But here all the booths are metal caravans. I smell sweet and savory, something baked, (auchooo) something smoky, and… something fresh? Tangy, like fruit! (hachoo) Sorry for all the sneezes, I guess I have some nose-overload. (sniffle) It's kind of dizzying to try to take it all in!"

Wandering the festival at a relaxed pace, Petrichor and Wynn point out and explain such marvels as food trucks, cell phones, cars, street lamps, electrical wires, cement (corrected from 'Seamint'), fire hydrants, debit cards and square readers. Eventually, with pretzel, tabbouleh, bubble tea, and poutine for sharing, the group finds a bench and a bit of grass to sit on and enjoy their snacks.

Briny plops down heavily, ready for a rest. "Even going at my own pace, this is exhausting! I'm definitely doing better than I was, though. Thank you for the crutches and guidance." Wynn smiles broadly while eating a forkful of cheesy, bacon-topped poutine fries, and reveling in the different tastes. Petrichor says, "We are happy to help!" while offering the tabbouleh and bubble tea. The sprite smiles and adds, "It's weird, though, how everyone looks so similar. I mean, we look just like everyone else! How do you even tell each other apart in a crowd?" Petrichor chuckles and answers, "Oh, I think it's like being anywhere new, really. It all seems a blur at first, but as you get used to it, it becomes easier to see the differences, tell people apart, and find your way around."

Facet sits on the end of the bench and continues looking through the journal with a nose-crinkle of concentration. Tonic sits on the grass, next to Briny's seat on the bench, and says with concern, "Hey Briny, I've noticed that Facet mostly follows along with the group, but never engages in conversation, and seems to somehow be in some different headspace than everyone else. What do you think is up?" The gnome fidgets and pats the moth plushie for reassurance.

Wynn looks a bit startled at this, and after hurriedly finishing the bite of poutine asks, "Is Facet's behavior new? I assumed it was just how Facet liked to interact."

Briny gives a worried huff. "Oh no, Facet isn't usually like this; Facet is generally energetic and out-going, full of ideas and sketches. This quiet, introspective, rock-obsessed Facet is new. Do you think this is like me losing the ability to get around?" The sprite gestures at the crutches.

Tonic looks melancholy, and takes out the moth plush: "Maybe. I feel like I've lost the thread of the story. We started this trip because of me; I wanted something new, I wanted to be different and interesting. It's been a wild time! But now I might have hurt my friends...again... and... maybe this isn't worth it? I'm really just supposed to be looking for Graemes. But Graemes always shows up at home again; eventually. I've had my adventure. I've finished my Wanderlust. Maybe we are done? I'd like to go home. How do you know when a story is done?"

Wynn corrects, "Hurt your friends?! Do you think you somehow caused these changes? You couldn't have. Facet's behavior isn't a *hurt*; it isn't bad! It is just a different way the brain functions, not something to be 'fixed.' Although, introversion and deep interest in topics aren't usually traits that happen suddenly; that part is unusual." Wynn shrugs with a smile, "One of the difficult things with quiet, introspective friends is that they don't speak up for themselves, and so they can easily get left out, or even be forgotten. So keep track of Facet, okay?" After a pause to make sure Tonic is paying attention, Wynn continues "Your friends are alright. These new situations may be troubling at first, but they aren't anyone's fault." Tonic nods and sneezes in reply.

Petrichor passes the bubble tea over to the gnome and adds, "You know, big adventures aren't for everyone. Epic quests are grand, but they aren't everyone's cup of tea. Different people need different adventures. For some people taking a boat to visit a cousin is a huge adventure, for others it is trying new food or doing a new job. Still others don't feel adventurous until they are hang-gliding off of a live volcano. Everyone is different. Travel changes all of us, and our travels are all different. Our 'ordinary' is all different." Tonic savors the sweet, creamy flavor of the bubble tea and enjoys the chewy boba bubbles. "I need to make a tea like this at home!" the gnome remarks. While the friends consider things, they trade their snacks around to ensure they each get a taste.

Wynn nods and adds, "I have always found that one of the fun things about having adventures and trying new things is getting to settle down and think about it all afterwords. Take time to remember and learn from the experience." Glancing at a bracelet on her wrist Wynn says, "Oh! I need to get to work. Thank you for the visit! Briny, are you okay now?" The EMT stands and dusts crumbs off her outfit.

"Yes, yes," the sprite assures everyone, "I can do okay now. Go do your job!" and Briny waves to Wynn while taking a big sip of the sweet, creamy boba tea.

Wynn hurries off, through the throng of people and food trucks. The festival is filling up. People walk or bike in, coming in groups of 1 to 5, then dispersing and re-forming with other groups. It is a bit like watching a chaotic but intricate dance.

Swaying gently side-to-side on the bench, Facet doodles little clouds, stones, ponds, gems, plants, clays, bowls, metals, and blankets next to various blobs in the once-birchbark journal. Briny hands over some snacks and says, "Facet? Eat something, okay?" Then the sprite breathes in deeply, trying to soak up all the excitement. The coblyn takes bites from the offered food while continuing to draw in the journal. Tonic stares off at the festival in a bittersweet mood.

Briny turns to Petrichor and asks, "Is Wynn a fairy who came over when very young?" the sprite pauses at using a new word, "...She... seems very used to Mythwold."

Petrichor's head shakes 'no.' "I think she's from here, but I'm not sure. I've never actually spoken to Wynn about the 'Fairyland'."

Briny continues the thought, "Tonic, could Wynn be in Graemes's journal?" which causes the gnome to yelp in reply, "Waugh! Curious Rituals!! I had forgotten! Where is it?!" Tonic begins feverishly rummaging through the peach pack. The gnome is bent over, scrabbling around in the pouches, "Augh!" The Mighty Teaspoon Hammer jangles in its sheath on the gnome's back, "What's happened to all our stuff?!"

Chapter 22: Finding

    Amid polleny puffs of sneezes and sniffles, Tonic searches for Curious Rituals of Uncommon Folk and other items. Briny looks through the seafoam satchel too. The gnome snuffles into a napkin, rubs an itchy palm, and takes a few deep breaths. "Okay, Graemes' journal is here, and Steam's travel teapot, a little bit of tea, some ceramic shards, but I don't see some of my other things. Although I do seem to now have this little...thing." Tonic holds up a small, rounded metal rectangle, with an ornate spoon etched on it.

    Petrichor nods, "Sometimes things disappear when you travel, and sometimes new stuff shows up. We call that a multi-tool here. It has a bunch of pieces that fold up small for easy carrying. It looks like yours has a knife, scissors, spoon, fork, and screwdrivers. They are very handy tools."

    Tonic practices using the multitool, and nervously pats at each hair puff. Facet sketches and sometimes taps or twiddles to an unknown beat; the coblyn's hair keeps falling forward, but Facet seems too focused to stop and adjust the goggles to use them as a headband. Briny finishes looking through the seafoam satchel; there are currently some shells, stale biscuits, and a handful of sand in the bottom. Around them, the food truck chefs call greetings and wave at passersby. The festival seems very popular, and many groups are sitting or standing around trying different dishes.

Briny sits and dances to the music and the roar of the food trucks. It is hot out, and the black road ensures that heat is amplified. Cultivated gardens have blooming flowers, and some birds and bugs explore there. The sprite notices lizards that watch from shaded spaces, and sometimes puff their throats and bob their heads.

Scratching a neck itch, Tonic puts away the mighty multitool (the gnome remains uncertain about naming the multitool; it hasn't really earned a capital-letter name yet), then opens Graemes's book. "Let's see if this helps; I just need to refocus. Maybe I can find how to get you home, and maybe there is a clue on how to find Graemes and finish up why we came here."

Other residents and guests bustle around the festival, which is quite lively. Briny sees kids playing games, and the place is full of chatter. Several people pause to watch Facet's sketchings, enjoying the art.

Rubbing both hands together to ease an itch, the gnome tries to decipher the journal entries, but is too tired and dejected to make any sense of them. The noises and colors are unfamiliar, and they make it difficult for Tonic to concentrate on the worn writing. The gnome cuddles the moth toy, then safely tucks it way in a petal-colored pocket of the overalls. Tonic takes another few bites of the poutine fries, thinking.

Briny is ecstatic at the fascinating new features that abound in this world, studying all different angles and experiences. While watching someone walking with their dog, the sprite suddenly gives a worried frown, and whistles for the windrabbits. It's been quite a long time since the windrabbits said hello, and they really should have come by for snacks and naps by now. Facet jiggles a leg and remains focused on studying rocks and on drawing.

Noticing the friends' downcast mood, Petrichor says, "Sometimes you are trying to keep track of so many things, you lose track of yourself. Tonic, it is good you care for your friends; remember that you are not a burden, your friends are choosing to stay with you. We are all choosing things minute to minute. You should each take a moment to focus on yourself, on your feelings...So what do you each want?"

Facet eats the last of the tabbouleh without looking up and whispers, "I miss my ideas," while sketching a slide next to an ink stain. The coblyn curls up smaller to keep out the hubbub of noise.

Briny looks at the crutches and says, "If it weren't for my mobility, I'd really like to stay and explore! Maybe if I can get used to this type of movement, I will stay a while. For now, I really want to help Tonic. ...And I'd really like to try whatever that is!" The sprite points to someone passing by, carrying a paper bowl filled with colorful swirls of creamy treats, sprinkled with bright flakes and topped with small pieces of vibrant fruit. Petrichor smiles hugely and says, "A sundae? Okay! I think that goal can be accomplished pretty quickly. We will clean up from these snacks, and then find the right food truck for that snack."

Tonic feels weirdly hot just as Briny yelps, "Tonic! Your face is all red and rash-y! Are you okay?"

"I'm fine." The gnome insists, "Just itchy. My neck and palms and lips itch a lot."

Petrichor throws away their trash, then has to explain the concept of single-use items, and throwing stuff away. Briny and Tonic are confused, and need the idea explained a few times. Tonic scratches at several itches. Briny looks dubious and twists a rainbow bracelet; "So, you make things to only use once, then stuff it in the ground because it doesn't go away, then take stuff out of the ground to make more?" the sprite asks. "That seems...odd."

Briny watches the skies for any sign of the windrabbits. Looking to see if they are hiding down low, the sprite suddenly spots Spindrift, Steam, and Turbine charms hanging out of Facet's bronze bag, just as Tonic realizes it is getting hard to breathe. "My tongue is too thick!" the gnome manages to say, while starting to panic.

A festival-goer stops to watch Facet draw, then says with a chuckle, "Well, hello!"

Chapter 23: Graemes

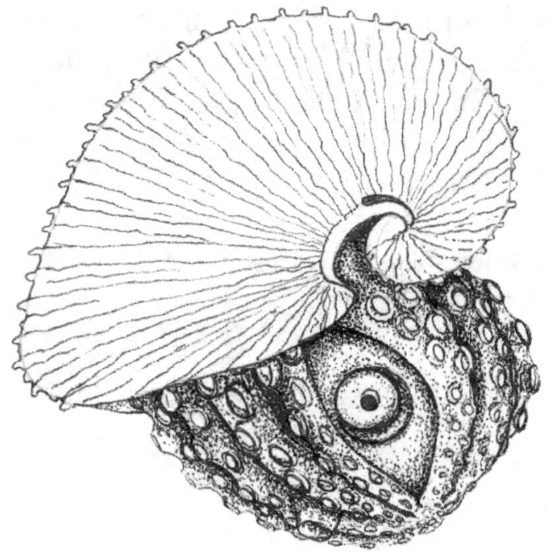

Graemes smiles, her peppery-white hair braided up in a bun, loose-fitting cotton overalls over a bright shirt, and oval glasses on her nose. "I didn't expect to see you here, Facet!"

Briny looks up and gasps, "Graemes!" Distracted from Facet's sketches by the shout and a glistening cloud of sneezes, Graemes looks up to see Tonic, Briny, and Petrichor. "Oh no! Tonic, you don't look well. It seems you Wildlings have discovered some new opportunities to face. Here, I have some allergy medicine that I think will help." Graemes digs around in an acorn-shaped leather bag and says, "Let's get Tonic something to drink. Water is probably best." Petrichor hurries off to buy a water, and Facet pauses sketching to put a small, speckled stone in Tonic's lap.

Once Tonic has swallowed the medicine, Graemes says in a business-like way, "Everyone okay? Is this your first trip into the World of Myth?" Briny nods. Their mentor continues, "That looks like a serious food allergy reaction *and* a pollen reaction. The medicine will help. I always keep some in my first aid kit. We *should* get Tonic to a hospital to ensure everything's okay, but as this is your first time here, you won't be able to prove you exist, and that's problematic."

Briny's mouth opens to object, "That's the stupidest..." Graemes holds up a hand, cutting off the thought and she says, "I know. Obviously you exist; you are right here. But sadly, the system they use here to allow you to be treated by healers requires extra proof. I think the best thing we can do right now is get Tonic inside and watch to ensure the medicine works."

Despite being anxious from the recent lack-of-breathing, Tonic sleepily nods and says, "I'm glad we found you, Graemes. Quest complete." before starting to doze off.

Sitting back inside Petrichor's apartment, Graemes says, "Quest complete? Were you three wandering around Mythwold just looking for me? Has something horrendous happened?!" As Briny quickly explains about the Wanderlust, and Tonic finding Graemes's book, and the trio's journey, Graemes listens and nods in understanding, "Ah, I see. Because of my musty old journal?!" Graemes laughs with an interrobang, "Quite the amazing tale!"

"Graemes?" Briny asks from a comfy spot on Petrichor's couch, "Why is the World's Between so frowned upon in Fierlund? At Tonic's Conclusion they were so concerned about the possibility of a Wildling! But I don't see how they present a real danger. And from what I understand, most never even learn about or make it across the World's Between!"

"Oh. Well," Graemes ponders, "Times change, I guess. There used to be many beings crossing the World's Between to and from Fierlund and Mythwold. But of course, there is always a price, like I said. I suppose some beings became fearful when loved ones came back changed, or didn't return at all. And over time, it became less and less 'good' or 'proper' to cross the World's Between. Then eventually it was a feared and hated thing to cross the World's Between, and slowly it turned into mere myths and was largely forgotten. The word 'Wildling' transformed from "someone who travels the World's Between" to simply "somebeing who misbehaves" and now Wildling is an almost forgotten word. Travel changes you, and traveling the World's Between always causes a change. Sometimes things change back, but sometimes they stay changed; and the longer you stay in one place or another the more you fit into that place. I think the idea of Wildlings traveling the World's Between is well on its way into the past, now; so few beings in Fierlund *or* Mythwold even remember that Wildlings and the World's Between are real. I'm pretty surprised anybeing thought of it at Tonic's Conclusion. Perhaps it was a half-remembered precaution left in the rules, or somebeing who knows me and my 'misbehavior' of traveling. "

Turning to Petrichor, Graemes says, "Thank you again. I really appreciate you taking care of my friends, and letting us use your place to watch over Tonic. The medicine generally makes the taker sleep for about 8 hours, so we are so very grateful to you for letting us stay here. How can we repay you?"

Petrichor smiles broadly, "Oh, it's a delight! I am enjoying chatting and hearing about home. The memories and stories are good payment. Maybe I'll even return one day. I wonder if I would get my old self back?"

Facet, worriedly sketching Turbine, quietly murmurs, "What changes back?"

Graemes looks somber and replies, "Travel always changes a being. I'm not entirely sure of all the rules of what changes and doesn't when you travel the World's Between. Generally, if it can exist in the place you go to, it seems to stay: like my journal. Or your Mighty Teaspoon Hammer. There are books here and it isn't a problem. On the other hand, while Tonic's Mighty Teaspoon Hammer is odd here in Mythwold, none of the science here actually opposes the existence of an enormous teaspoon hammer. But things that *can't* exist *must* change to fit the rules of the world: mammals here cannot be part plant, so Tonic's mossy, bark-like gnome skin changes. The same sort of changes happened to Facet's gem hair and Briny's splashy waves. Beings that are enough like humans become more human, beings that are more like animals become that animal, and some beings change to match either their form, substance, or purpose. And sometimes, stuff just goes missing or turns up. I find that last part to be true whenever you move residence, anywhere in either world. I assume there is some sort of spell, or largely unstudied creature, that takes, gives, and generally rearranges stuff when anybeing moves houses."

Briny speaks up, "Graemes, having an adventure, finding you; this was all Tonic's Wanderlust. Now that you are here, I'm not sure what's next. How do we get home? Do we go? Do we stay in this fantasy land?"

Graemes pauses thoughtfully and adds, "You said Tonic is ready to go home. Getting back is never quite the same as going out, on any journey. Sometimes you can take the same path, but rarely. Some doors to the World's Between stay stationary, like maybe a path in the woods or a particular book, but some change, like a ring of mushrooms popping up one night and elsewhere the next. I usually follow the Changing Wind." Facet sketches a picture of a happy breeze, as Graemes goes on, "The Changing Wind isn't easy to pin down a time or location that you will find it. In fact, part of the Changing Wind is that it happens rather unexpectedly. It is a cool breeze after hot days, or the warm, earthy, morning gust after cold. For traveling the World's Between I find the Changing Wind when it is a breeze like the ocean, and I follow it."

Briny looks up, grinning, and says, "I know that wind! It's a cool evening wind, with edges of heat clinging to it. It feels like sunburns and sea spray, like calling gulls and fresh tomato sandwiches. Like warm nights and rainbow sunsets with clouds racing away. Like grill outs and ghost crabs, and what shore creatures you can find first thing in the morning. Like sand between your toes."

Graemes nods with a wistful laugh, "Yes, indeed! That is the Changing Wind that calls me to the ocean, where I sail to Fierlund, Fairyland, the Land of Legends, and back to Mythwold, the World of Myth." After a slight pause, Graemes continues reassuringly, "Once Tonic wakes up, we will get you all sorted on what to do next."

Chapter 24: Fierlund

While the tea gnome sleeps, Graemes and Petrichor take
turns watching over Facet, Briny, and Tonic. The group chats,
naps, and even gets the sought-after sundae from the festival.
The Quest for the Sundae is but a small, simple quest. It is
easily completed with the knowledgeable Petrichor in the
lead.

Briny is instantly enamoured of the cold, creamy treat.
The sprite gushes, "This is a delight! Smooth, but with
crunchy bits. A beautiful swirl and bright color flecks to look
at, with rivers of warm chocolate. And all of it wrapped in
sweet, delectable flavors! I have *got* to learn how to make
it." Graemes and Petrichor agree that sundaes are delicious.
Back at Petrichor's apartment, Facet tries a small bite of
sundae when a spoonful is offered, but the coblyn decides
the textures and temperature are too much, and curls up in
a corner. Tonic continues to sleep, the rash slowly goes away,

and the gnome seems able to breathe easily again.

Briny tells the story of their adventures so far, filling Graemes in about Tonic's Wanderlust, and how they ended up in the World of Myth. As the group is getting drowsy and ready to sleep, Briny plays with the windrabbit charms that hang out of the bronze bag. Each charm is attached to a different fancy pen; Turbine hangs off an intricate metallic pen, Steam is on a detailed wooden pen, and Spindrift hangs off a pen with a tiny glass window where pictures of windrabbits and Sea Bunnies slosh back and forth in water. "Are these really our windrabbits? Have they actually been transformed into tiny charms?" the sprite asks with a shake that jangles their rainbow bracelets.

Graemes looks sorrowful and replies, "I don't know, Briny. I've never seen a windrabbit manifest before, and I've never brought one through the World's Between; Mythwold science doesn't allow for living rabbits made of wind." Seeing the sprite's fearful expression, Graemes adds, "They probably were transformed, but I don't know if they will stay charms forever. Very likely they will change back when you return to Fierlund, but it's never certain. For example, I'm all tangled up in my own time, and that won't change. And my own friend Villepreux changed the first time we traveled to Fierlund from here in Mythwold; originally she was a charming, folded paper-toy octopus, but she changed into a living, thinking paper nautilus (which is a type of octopus that lives in the open ocean); she has never changed back into a paper toy, but when we return to the World of Myth she becomes a cozy houseboat. Sometimes in travels we are only changed for a time, sometimes we are changed for life."

After Briny, Facet, and Petrichor all fall asleep, Graemes goes to the window and watches the bats come out and fly across the night sky. Sitting and watching, Graemes wonders, "What ultimately happens to the windrabbits? Does only Briny's turn back, being more strongly connected to the sprite? Will Tonic feel a friendly breeze in the tea garden sometimes, or Facet treasure a cavern gust? Will they remain pen charms forever?...I wonder why pen charms?"

With a heavy sigh, Graemes rubs tired eyes, trying to get rid of the blurriness and translucent 'floaters' that disrupt vision. "Oof. What good is getting old? What good is age? What good is seeing the nuances of things, just as our eyesight leaves us? What good is understanding the lessons, just as we no longer need them?"

Petrichor murmurs sleepily, "I used to have a friend named Clover. I miss running errands together; it was our favorite time to visit. I should see if I can send a letter..." And so they all drift off to sleep, perchance sorting out their thoughts in dreams.

In the morning the group makes plans for getting home. Petrichor noses around the pantry, and makes oatmeal with nuts and frozen berries for everyone. Enjoying the warm morning meal, Tonic is still slightly groggy, but feels otherwise in good health. "Graemes, I'm really glad I found you, and that you are well. I've been using your journal as an inspiration and a guide; Would you like it back? I'm glad to have had my adventure, and am ready to go back home. Will you be coming with us?"

With a head-shake and a pat on the shoulder, Graemes explains, "No, not yet. Villepreux wants to visit the Sydney Opera House. She's certain it's an ancient paper nautilus shell, and wishes to see if the Argonauta argo is still around there somewhere. But I will keep in mind that it has been a while, and try to visit soon."

Briney reminds Graemes to visit Nightshade, and pays Petrichor with coins from home: a Bean, a Glamour, and a Pot. The tylwyth teg says thanks to the sprite with a big, squeezy hug, "You needn't pay anything, but these are a great memento of home. Thank you!"

Tonic turns to Petrichor and says, "Thank you so much for all of your help and kindness! I'm not sure how to fully repay it all. This adventure has been amazing, and I've learned a lot of things! I've seen so much and thought so many new things, and I truly appreciate your help here in Mythwold!" Looking around the room, the tea gnome nervously continues, "But I'm ready to go home. This world is too much! It feels too strange and perilous for me to be comfortable here. Briny can't walk, and Facet can't even communicate if they *want* to stay or not. And I'm in peril just from eating and breathing! Our quest is complete, let's wrap it up in a book of memories like Wynn suggested, and think about it all back at home."

Briny looks up in horrified surprise and tries hard to catch a thousand fleeting thoughts and feelings, "Why would we go back home, Tonic? That's just... ordinary stuff! But **this**; this is amazing! There is magic, and astounding things *everywhere*! There are sundaes, and cars, and phones, and internet; there is energy flying through the air *all over* Mythwold! I haven't experienced or understood half of the words I've learned here, and that's a miniscule portion of the things there are to learn about in Mythwold!"

Confounded by Briny's enthusiasm to stay in the World of Myth, it takes the gnome a moment to answer; "Are you *sure*, Briny? What about tidal traffic? A fluffle of windrabbits and Sea Bunnies? Storm Chasing with your cousin? This adventure has been so big, so... well, so *much*! How will you even get around if you can't walk?!" Anxiously rooted to the spot, Tonic continues, "This whole Wanderlust has shown me just how much there is for me to explore back in Fierlund! There is so much I don't know about our home. And I *want* to go home, back to my gardens. I want to go back, I want a chance to rest at my comfortable teapot, and then, maybe later I want to discover more about *our* land. ... Don't you?"

Briny looks shocked at the idea and bursts out, "leaving all of Mythwold just to go home?!"

Pausing for a breath, Tonic continues, "I think I've learned something important on this Wanderlust, I've learned that I really do enjoy adventures. Small, safe ones. Something where I can learn something new, but not too far outside my usual and known. In addition, well, I really do want to go back and be a Steeper. All that effort and fuss over Conclusions; I'd hate to waste my opportunities." finishes Tonic.

With bafflement, Briny bursts out, "What? No! Our Craft Courses and Conclusions were great, sure! I learned a lot, I studied hard and proved to myself what I can do. But this... this is a chance to learn so much more! Sure, I can go home and be a Storm Chaser or something, but here I can experience totally new things; that's just what makes Mythwold so exciting! Our own Fierlund is so vast, and yet *here's* a place with completely *different* rules, and where magic is *real*!" With a glance at Petrichor, the sprite continues, " ...Or, at least, their science works differently. How can you not be inspired to stay and understand all that's here? It's amazingly, refreshingly new!" Full of hope, the sprite turns to Graemes and asks, "Can I stay here? May I travel with you, Graemes?"

"Yes, if you want." Graemes replies to Briny, then asks the sprite, "Are you okay with adventure and peril and weird, new things?"

"Yes!" Briny bubbles, "Are you willing to help me with my mobility for our adventures?"

Graemes twinkles, "That sounds like some added interest to our excitement! However, it's bound to be frustrating and boring sometimes."

"That's okay," Briny shrugs with a jangle of rainbow bracelets, "Tonic says it is good to have time to breathe and assess. And if it was all fun and easy, I might forget it was fun and easy, right? It's good to have perspective shifts."

Petrichor speaks up, "Tonic, how will you and Facet get home?" Momentarily stunned, the gnome isn't sure how to respond, just blinks and stares while trying to think up a solution.

Graemes and Briny give Tonic time to ponder as they start to chat about travel plans and what to pack. Before Tonic is able to come up with a reply to Petrichor's question, Facet whispers, "Follow your star" repeatedly while petting a small, star-shaped box. "Follow your star; follow your star..."

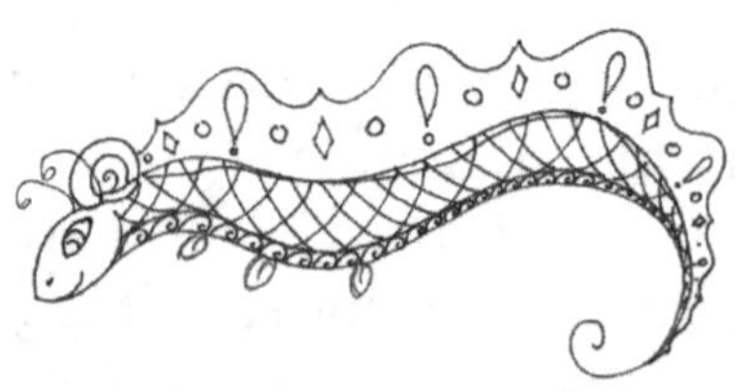

Chapter 25: Going Home

Tonic blinks in confusion, "What was that Facet?" The gnome looks over at the coblyn's journal, and sees a page with sketches of a tent, a boat, and a sandwich. Facet continues holding the little box and swaying gently. The coblyn's thoughts sizzle and rocket; boats, across the sky, shooting stars, gears turning, sad Tonic made happy, best sandwiches, Clickfish in the cave, and a thousand more things… but Facet can only repeat, "Follow your star."

Turning, Tonic says, "Petrichor, I really don't know how we will get home. Can't we just walk back up the trail we came in?" The tylwyth teg looks pensive. "Well, that might work, but it usually doesn't. Not only is it a journey to go through the World's Between one way, it's usually a journey to get back, too. And although the path from the Snail's Gift clearly leads *here*, if it were easy to get back that way I would have gone long ago."

"How do you usually get back?" Tonic queries.

Petrichor's shoulders sag, "I haven't ever gone back. At first I was freaked out, and couldn't even think well enough to figure out how to get back. Later, when I could think more clearly, I had made friends, like Wynn, and a home, and I wanted to keep exploring this world. ...and I'm uncertain of what I would find. I haven't *really* tried to find my way back."

Graemes adjusts the conversation, saying, "There are Lintels here, but the Marginalia that protect them are different. I've seen Lintels that are vine tunnels, trains, gaps between trees, unexpected alleys, burrows in the ground, or even fancy desserts; but I've not witnessed the Marginalia, the Lintels just seem to hide. While Fierlund has Lintels well protected by obvious Marginalia puzzles and guards, here in Mythwold I've never actually seen any Marginalia. Some say a dragon or a minotaur built a giant, shifting, invisible maze and made it one big Marginalia for all the Lintels in Mythwold. That's why I always follow the Changing Wind, and why my trips in Mythwold are never a set length of time."

Tonic's jaw is set firm, "Okay; we can figure out Lintels in a minute. We will need some way to sleep safely on the way home... OH! The Night Tent! Briny; doesn't the Night Tent become a boat? Do you think Facet and I can sail home, like Graemes does?" Tonic turns and gives Facet a proud hug, "That's what you were trying to tell me, isn't it? You have your journal open to the sketches of the Night Tent, and it folds up into a star - I bet that box you are holding is the Night Tent! That's what we will use to start our journey home."

Facet smiles, holding the star-shaped box, and twiddling the rocks laying on the open journal; the rocks are finally in the right order. It's okay now. With a content sigh, the coblyn murmurs, "Second star to the right... follow your star... star light, star bright."

After many lingering thanks, and some securely wrapped snacks from Petrichor, the groups depart. Petrichor gifts

Tonic, Facet, Graemes, and Briny each a knitted flower, and a self-addressed stamped envelope, hoping this will allow them to stay in touch. "What a clever idea!" Graemes enthuses, "I never thought to see if postal letters could cross the World's Between! Splendid idea, and happy to give it a try. Maybe the windrabbit ink will help the letters find their way, what do you think, Briny?" The sprite's blue eyes sparkle at the idea. Petrichor happily gives Briny the crutches, glad they will be useful again.

Briny puts the pens with the charms of Steam and Turbine into Tonic's peach pack, with a cheerful pat and breezy smile. Facet silently gives everybeing a stone with solemnity, Graemes hugs them all robustly, and Tonic (with eyes bright and glassy with unshed tears) portions out the last of the tea packed from home, giving each being an equal share.

Buoyed and ebullient, Graemes and Briny head off to a station of carriages called buses, ready for new and interesting things to do and learn; the sprite's rainbow bracelets jingle and swish with energy. From there, they will return to where Villepreux is docked, and have a long, winding journey sailing to Australia, where they can check on the nautilus-ness of the Sydney Opera House.

Petrichor walks Tonic and Facet back to the unfinished neighborhood they entered from. There is no freshening wind, no feeling they want to follow, but there is a natural lake. Petrichor must go to work, so leaves Facet and Tonic to their travels with hugs and smiles. Gnome and coblyn try to plan how to set sail for home in the Night Tent. Especially as said tent is currently a small, star-shaped box.

"I hope we don't need an ocean, Facet, because this lake is what we've got." Tonic says, checking that the sun has set fully before placing the star-shaped box on the water. "And I really hope we don't end up with a soggy sandwich."

After watching the box bob up and down on the water,

and do nothing else, Facet reaches out and pulls a small cord that had gone unnoticed. With a good tug, then several more, the box finally opens, expanding several compartments into a large inflatable raft with a sunshade. The gnome loads their gear, steps squealchily aboard, and helps Facet in. The inflatable raft is only about 2 gnomes long, and 1.5 gnomes wide. Tonic looks around the raft: the sunshade is a pale blue like the sky, and the inflated base of the raft is colored like a sandwich, sort of a bread-y tan, with a darker 'crust' color around the edges; and looking over the side Tonic sees stripes of leaf-y green, tomato-y read, and egg-y yellow-white. The gnome pats the boat, happy that while their raft may be a sandwich, at least it is meant to be soggy. With bare feet and drying toes, the two friends set out for the distant horizon.

Tonic and Facet drift slowly for some time, paddling as best they can with their hands or bits of branches, and the Mighty Teaspoon Hammer. Facet doesn't concentrate well on this task, and soon goes to check their packs and things. It isn't long before the coblyn is falling asleep under the raft's shade, with small items organized by color, size, and shape, in rows and piles all around. The improvised rowing is difficult and tiring, and Tonic eventually falls asleep thinking of the sketches of the Night Tent; in the dream, Tonic is being pursued by an angry swan, the gnome keeps trying to kick it, then falls and ends up confined, like a gift wrapped in ribbons.

In the pre-dawn morning, the raft is much improved, and appears to have settled into the idea of being a small houseboat. Delighted with this find, Tonic tumbles out of a hammock, and goes to make tea in the tidy kitchen. Facet wakes up from among their gear, and flaps frantically out the window, while making garbled, half-formed noises. Trying to avoid Facet's flailing hands, Tonic accidentally spills hot water and shouts at Facet, "Stop waving your hands about!

Just tell me what you want, already!"

Facet stops, and looks blankly at Tonic. The coblyn quickly looks down, and shifting weight from one foot to the other, Facet gestures slightly toward the window. An enclosure of castles looms up at them quickly as their boat runs aground with a shuddering jerk, and a terrible scrunching noise.

Tonic softens and apologizes, "I'm sorry for when I sound mean, Facet; I really don't intend to be. I'm just worried, and anxious. I want to be kind and helpful, but sometimes I just freak out instead. I need to work on that." Facet continues to look at the floor, and Tonic huffs in frustration, muttering, "I really wish I could tell if you understood me."

Tonic looks out the window again, to see the dark clouds, with bellies low and growling, and the sun just trying to rise. The gnome of tea, having traveled so far from home, wonders, "Are we lost in the World's Between? Like the Snail's Gift? Or are we still in Mythwold?..."

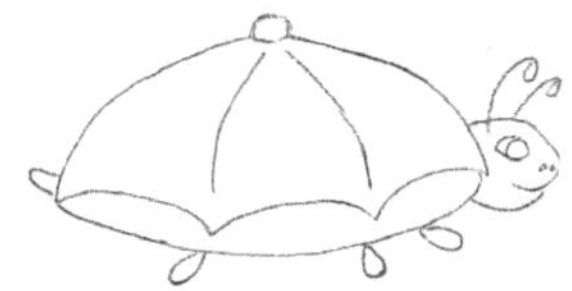

Chapter 26: Castledom

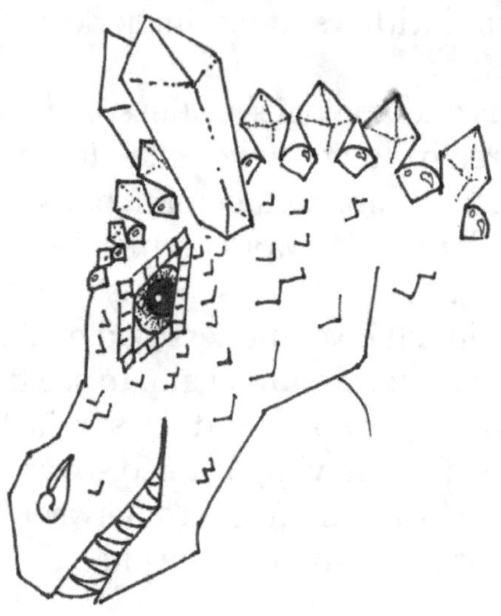

Tonic encourages Facet out onto the pebbly shore. "We certainly aren't in the small pond near Petrichor anymore. Do you think we are back in Fierlund?"

Facet takes a deep breath, appears to try to answer with fingers twining and tapping, then squints at the trees, looks down at their fluttering hands, and finally shrugs with a head shake.

"Well, let's see where we are then." After securing the Night Tent boat, Tonic leads the way towards the enormous castle, "I wish Briny were here to help with those clouds; they look ominous. At least the air is cooler now, like proper autumn."

Facet hums as they walk along the shore and into the forest thicket. They fight bracken and briars, and collect a fair amount of stings and scratches on the way. When they finally reach the castle, they aren't sure how to proceed. Tonic tries knocking on the heavy wooden door, but after waiting, no one answers. Looking for some bell or knocker,

Tonic feels soft kisses from the sky.

Big, fat drops of rain begin to *splut* onto the ground, leaving tiny, muddy ponds in the dirt. The raindrops play a soft, rustling tune as they hit the leaves, quickening to an impossible jig as it really starts to pour.

Drenched, itchy, and sore Tonic decides to barge into the castle, and ask for forgiveness if necessary. Desperately hoping the door isn't locked, the gnome of tea shoves on the door and stumbles into the foyer.

Somebeing emerges from another room, blinking green eyes in surprise at the disgruntled Tonic and Facet. "Hmm. Let's get you cleaned up, then. On a Wanderlust, are we?" The young figure leads the two friends into a kitchen, where mugs of warm mint tea are made, towels brought for cleaning and drying, and first aid given to scratches, stings, and bites. The being, Driftwood, is a youthful rusalka with blue-swirled skin, webbed fingers, and long, kelp-like hair. The rusalka starts the introductions and explains that the friends have found their way to Castledom, where the surrounding forest sometimes connects to the World's Between.

Once everybeing is tended to, and far less bedraggled, Tonic explains to Driftwood about their journey to get home. "Driftwood, how did you know we were on a Wanderlust? And can you help us get home? We live near the Bloomiary and Apis Distillery."

Driftwood's long jacket ("or is it a robe?" Facet wonders, while doodling on the tabletop with a finger. "What defines a jacket or robe? What about a cloak? Can it be a trenchcoat?") rustles slightly at their feet as the rusalka launches enthusiastically into explaining what they know, "Well, as heir to the Castledom, I must be well-versed in many things! I'm sure I've heard of the Bloomiary. There are, of course, geographic studies, and lessons on nations and cultures, language classes, dancing and deportment for grace, tutors on war, poisons, and personal combat, graphs on economic progressions, lectures about the country's needs and trends in jobs, trades, and commerce, history interwoven throughout, and practical lessons on problem solving! And, of course, the forest sometimes turns out beings on a Wanderlust. We've always helped them." Driftwood beams hopefully, waiting for the visitors to be impressed. Facet returns the smile, and pushes a sketch of the trio having tea towards the young Rusalka. "Thank you!" Driftwoods exclaims at the gift. The rusalka hops up and rushes to a window as a burst of firelight glows from outside. "Come look at this! We have recently set up some great Dragon Drop technology! We have been training dragons to deliver packages, but only recently discovered how to get them to drop things where we want them to. Dragons see differently than we do and we are trying a series of colored marks only they see. The colors on their packages match the color of the X painted on the ground! Amazing, isn't it?! Some of the dragons let out a flame after dropping their parcels."

Tonic watches a few dragons practicing in the courtyard and wonders if the dragons flame from frustration or happiness. The creatures bound over to a large pile of crates, pick one up in their talons, flap high into the air, and after circling a moment, they drop the crates in different areas. There doesn't seem to be rhyme nor reason to which dragons flame and which don't. The garden gnome has no idea if the boxes are going to the right spot, but is suitably impressed with the dragons' training. "That is amazing!" Tonic agrees.

The pale circle of the sun glows faintly from behind the dark clouds, and the household of Castledom starts to wake up. There is shuffling and rustling from other rooms as beings start their day. "Come with me, to see where you are! That might help you find the way you need to head home. You are at least in Fierlund now, so that's progress." Driftwood dashes out onto a landing, and up a set of stairs outside.

Tonic and Facet follow. Once up the stairs, the friends look around and catch their breath. Examining the area, Tonic sees they are on a smallish island, situated in the middle of a lake. The castle is to one side of the island, and the forest takes up the middle space, with a stream flowing through it. There are several bridges spanning the stream at different points. The far side of the island seems to have tall hills or short mountains. Facet takes a rubbing of the castle stones, labels the impressions, and mutters the names of different stones. Neither friend knows how to get home from here.

While looking at the scenery, Facet's hands start to flutter like birds. Tonic looks at the coblyn in concern, trying to decide what to do.

"Oh look! It's the Overmorrow balloon!" Driftwood squeaks with excitement, pointing to the sky.

Looking up to follow the gaze of Facet and Driftwood, Tonic sees a distant, rainbow-colored dot among the dark clouds. As they watch, the rain lessens, the grey clouds turn paler, and the bright rainbow dot gets bigger.

Driftwood does a happy dance and shouts, "Let's go say hi! I love when the twins visit!"

Curtains are opening in the castle, beings move about doing chores, and Driftwood races to the shore at the base of the Castledom. Tonic and Facet scramble to keep up with the exuberant rusalka, slipping some and not as sure-footed as the waterbeing. When they reach the ground, the two friends see the cheerful globe of Weathervane's hot air balloon floating in to land nearby!

Tonic waves up to Weathervane with joy and relief at seeing not just a friendly face, but one who can help them get home! Tonic drags Facet well out of the way, and then goes to pack up the Night Tent. Facet adjusts the goggles, then breathes slowly while counting the stones in their pockets. In Tonic's eagerness to get home, an important detail is forgotten... the gnome returns to the hot air balloon with a squashed sandwich that is shaped like a boat. "Sorry, Facet"

Tonic winces, "I'll put it away carefully, and hopefully it will open back out correctly at night." Facet takes the squashed Night Tent sandwich with a nod, and carefully tucks it into the Bronze Bag.

Weathervane cries, "Fairwinds and a view-hallew to everybeing on the shore!"

Driftwood gives Weathervane a hug, then noses around the balloon, commenting on all the new things since last they met. The rusalka happily grabs some letters out of the balloon's basket, then hurries off to grab more letters in exchange. After Driftwood rushes off to get the letters, Tonic asks, "Weathervane, how are you? It's so good to see you! Can you please help us get home? Is Compass here? Are you stopping to tell stories?"

With a chuckle, Weathervane offers hugs to both gnome and coblyn, responding, "I'm actually here to pick you up! I was using the Useful Device you gave me last time we met, and I happened to see you over here in Castledom. Figured you might want a lift. Did you find your Graemes?" Facet nods and shifts weight from one foot to the other.

Driftwood bounds back, dropping letters, rebounding to grab them, and bounding back toward Weathervane. "I'm so stoked you're back! Can I ride Overmorrow while you're here?!" the rusalka wonders.

"Not this time, my friend." Weathervane answers. I need Overmorrow to take these two as far back to their homes as I can." Driftwood looks crestfallen, then perks back up, "But next time, I can *steer*?"

Weathervane lets out a loud guffaw and agrees, "You drive a hard bargain, but yes, I think you can steer a bit next time I visit." Driftwood rushes off shouting the news to the Castledom, and only belatedly turns to wave, "Until we meet again! May it be soon!"

Weathervane, Facet, and Tonic wave to the rusalka, then gather up their things and board the balloon.

Chapter 27: Overmarrow

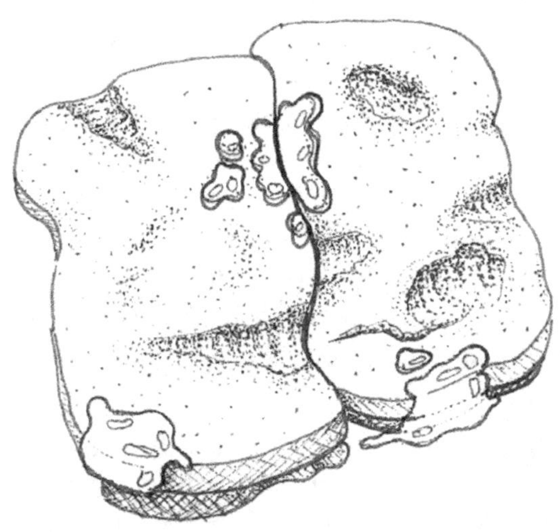

The basket base is a big and sturdy room, and the three friends fit snugly. The flight is cozy as they drift up through the shadowed, cloudy skies, and Tonic's body fills with relief. Facet finishes writing their names and addresses on a sheet from the birchbark, then carefully tears it out and folds it like a whirligig seed, dropping it down to the Casteldom below. Pulling the goggles up to act like a hairband, the coblyn watches the paper twirl toward the ground.

"What a great idea, Facet!" Tonic crows, "If we pass over any more of our friends, we should drop them notes so we can send each other letters!"

For a long while Tonic and Weathervane share stories. Tonic and Facet learn that Weathervane's balloon, Overmorrow, got its naming from the Nightjar's idea that a journey should always go on until the day after tomorrow.

All three friends watch the skyscapes and the landscapes

changing below them for many lengths; the world looks a bit like a crescent moon in a deep sky. They chat with enthusiasm, watch the geography pass by, and eat sparsely, rationing their meals. Weathervane points out areas of interest, "We are in Fief right now, this country is filled with castles, and the winds are blowing away from Saltwave, so we are likely to see the cities and lights of Gearlock. We might even blow so far as Confection'ry."

Tonic's hair puffs have their leafy-green tips back, and their beautiful bark skin has returned too, though most of the used-to-be-mossy patches are still bare and pale. Examining their clothes, the gnome pats their faithful brown and green outfit's brightly stitched leaf patterns (noticing that they have more dirt, sweat, and tea stains than they began with). Facet's skin looks more like swirled clay and jade again, and the coblyn's green eyes shimmer with silver again too. The trio floats on; there are hills and fields, lakes, farms, mountains, storms, clouds, and clear skies. And late one afternoon, Facet even joins in naming cloud shapes in the sky.

"A majestic turtle-dragon," Tonic says, indicating a cloud slightly to the right.

"Very nice! Hmm." Weathervane waves to clouds on the left, "A mighty battle between seastar and duck." Tonic nods approvingly.

"Gems," Facet whispers, pointing at a cluster of clouds ahead.

"You're right Facet! Those do look like gems. What other cloudshapes do you see?" Tonic asks with gentle surprise. Weathervane notes heat lightning ahead, stabbing from cloud to cloud, and takes the helm to steer the balloon craft away.

Facet's eyes gleam and the coblyn starts to rattle off shapes, pointing at clouds everywhich way, almost as fast as their tumbling thoughts, "cumulo. Heart. Bat. Lantern. Whale chasing a flower. Potion bottles and tea cake! My meal table. Bubbles of Clickfish. Bramble!"

Tonic's mouth hangs open as Facet continues, "How do you think Clickfish travel? Could they be housed in potion bottles? I know they like my caves, and the clinking of your tea. Would Castledom still be a castle if it was glass? What kind of flowers would a whale chase? Do you have a favorite flower? I think mine might be Stonecrop. Maybe saxifrage or wood sorrel; they grow near caves, you know."

While Weathervane directs Overmorrow past the storm, Tonic bursts out, "Facet! You can talk! You...are YOU again! What happened?"

"Tonic," Facet starts with a worried frown, eyes flashing hidden blue-green hues, "I'm still me; I've always *been* me. In Mythwold I had so many thoughts, and every single thing was so overwhelming, SO overwhelming, I just couldn't communicate; but I was always *me*. Now, I still have a hundred new ideas, zapping through my thoughts. Only, now... well, I can't seem to write them down and be productive with them as easily. They spark so fast, rocketing from one thought to the next, it's often hard to hold a coherent conversation; I often end up with seeming non-sequitors, because my ideas have jumped and connected to other thoughts. I certainly can't always write my ideas down fast enough to remember them later!" Facet's hands start to fidget and flap. "But, yes, I *do* still have a lot of good ideas. Ideas all the time! Just flicking past, faster than a hummingbird's wing. I just need to figure out how to remember them and organize them so I can be usefully productive on them. Like, how do clouds get shaped? Are they creatures, or can we build shaped clouds? I wish I could keep a cloud to help me remember! Also, we really need to get everything secured."

Tonic gives Facet a big hug, overjoyed to be able to communicate again. "Oh, it is so good to hear you again, and know you understand me. I've missed talking with you!"

"Yes," Facet agrees while crouching down, "I like being

able to communicate, but I really think we should hold on.”

"Good to hear you again!" Weathervane calls over one shoulder. "This storm is a bit bigger than I thought. I'm going to set us down to wait it out." Overmorrow rocks a bit in the turbulent wind. "You might want to hold on to anything important!" Weathervane calls while making the balloon dodge around the rough skies. Tonic joins Facet and together they try to hold on to all the items already rattling and skittering around.

Once they land in a field, (less of landing, and more of a tumultuous, tumbling, crash which digs up furrows) they take stock. Once things are un-jumbled, they find that the Spray Slip (for slippers) has slid over the side, the Stop Flop (for better flips) has flattened, and a receipt for Quiet Classes (for sneakers) has snuck away. Everything else seems to be fine.

The rain lashes down as Weathervane, Facet, and Tonic all try to stay dry under an overhang, with Overmorrow secured nearby. While the exhausted friends wait out the storm, Facet talks about the rocks collected from Mythwold, and the memories connected to each. Tonic uses the Mighty Teaspoon Hammer as an extra shield against the storm as they all begin falling asleep.

In the morning the storm herd has passed, and using the Useful Device to see further, Weathervane spots Compass heading their way. Weathervane goes to meet Compass and they walk back to the friends together, while Facet and Tonic lay out what items they can to dry on some large rocks. The coblyn checks the oakcorn basket for cracks, but it is secure and the contents inside are dry.

Facet greets Compass with enthusiastic questions about the landscape (Are we anywhere near the Silverwood?"), geography (are you headed toward a river? Or a mountain?"), and other land-bound delights ("Do you always travel roads, or do you make your own path? How many boulders have you climbed? Do you ever go into caves?"). "It's just that we've been on the water, and we've been in the sky, and it's really good to be back on the ground!" the coblyn concludes.

"Yes, I've seen the Silverwood; I'm headed over the hills and toward the Pebbling Plain; I usually travel roads, but I do sometimes forge my own; and of course!" Compass replies, "You should travel with me for a while. You can keep your feet on the ground that way."

Facet picks up a shiny quartz stone and turns to Tonic, "What do you think? Shall we walk a bit?"

The gnome of tea looks around, and up at the sky, and thinks of home. "I don't know, Facet. Aside from that storm-landing, I think taking Overmorrow is much faster. And I'm worried about Bramble and my gardens, and I ache, and I could do with a long soak and a change of clothes." Tonic hesitates, then lets out a rush of air. "I'm very ready to get home, I think."

Facet looks crestfallen, but Compass chirps, "Oh good! We will each have a companion. Facet can come with me, and Tonic can go with Weathervane. We can all meet up again by the Seasons' Shore. What do you think?"

"Excellent idea!" Weathervane chuffs.

They spend the day drying out and foraging. Facet keeps getting distracted by cool rocks, interesting tree bark, pretty flowers, and fantastic stones, so delighted to be on the ground. Tonic cheers up finding some great chicken-of-the-woods mushrooms, beechnuts, asparagus, and sage. Once all ingredients are gathered, dusted, washed, chopped, and cooked, it is turned into a hearty lunch stew for all of them, with a bit extra laid out to dehydrate for use later. Their clothes and things dry in the sun on the warming rocks, and for a while everybeing is content. Tonic even catches a whiff of the sweet-smelling Steam. Chuckling at the gusty nuzzle on their leafy-green hair puffs, the gnome calls, "Facet! I think the WindRabbits are back!"

A quick search of the bronze bag and peach pack prove the rabbit charms are missing, and in their place are the pens and broken bits of collars instead. "Turbine, if you're about, can you help keep Overmorrow aloft and well-steered?" Facet asks the air. The balloon rustles, and they all take that as a good sign. "Oh crumbs;" Tonic murmurs, "I guess we can't see Steam or Turbine until Briny gets back."

Chapter 28: Up While Down

The group spends a more comfortable night, with a fire to keep them warm in the crisp night air, and no rain soaking them through. Tonic cleans the Mighty Teaspoon Hammer, and gives it a thankful pat, "I'm so glad to have my Teaspoon! It scooped a perfect divot for our fire pit." The fire also helps dry out anything that was still damp. The group sits around the fire singing old songs and making up new ones, and finishing the last of their saved provisions.

Facet addresses the Nightjar Twins, "I appreciate you helping me gather rocks for the fire ring. Now let's see if my squashed sandwich is ready to work again!" Shaking out the soggy sandwich Night Tent, the coblyn adds, "This is such a Very Useful Device! It was too wet and squishy yesterday, and I couldn't get it to stop being a sandwich."

Weathervane and Compass watch with polite curiosity as Facet twists and shakes the sandwich, until suddenly it unfolds with a clothy *pop*. And there before them is the Night Tent: a slightly bent side where it's minus one star, smelling of walnuts and honey, and gloriously cozy and dry! Watching it fade into the landscape, the coblyn leads the way inside. As the Nightjars marvel at the glorious colors inside, Tonic hops jubilantly into one of the four snug beds. Burrowing under the covers, the gnome refuses to come out until morning. Facet, Compass, and Weathervane bring the bags, packs, and other items inside, then settle down for a restful night's sleep.

The next nearly-morning Facet wakes up in the pre-dawn light and ensures everybeing is up and out of the Night Tent before the sun sheds its full light on the day, "Get up! Time to be awake and alert! This tent will be untenable in no time! Out, out, out!" The coblyn's hair has it's quartzey texture back, and garnet glimmers too, and although Facet's eyes are still grey-green, they look more like labradorite now (with blue-green hues winking on and off as the light shifts). Surprisingly, the coblyn's large, round, gem-studded goggles (the ones with smoked-glass lenses) have made it into Mythwold and back to Fierlund without getting lost or broken; they are certainly dirtier, and some gems have fallen out, but they are still quite serviceable. Facet currently uses them as a headband, since no vine is handy for a hair tie.

With amusement, the Nightjar Twins gather up their respective belongings, and refresh Overmorrow until the balloon is ready to fly. Tonic asks Steam to help find some food, although the windrabbit still cannot be seen, while Facet twists and folds the Night Tent back into a small, portable star.

After the others are ready, and everything is packed and properly apportioned, Tonic comes back with some apples, water lily roots, and more asparagus all bulging out of the peach pack; it's late in the year for asparagus, but the gnome is pleased to have it. Steam brings more beechnuts, or so they assume, as they see the seeds juggling in the breeze behind Tonic. The friends divide up the food supplies, and start on their separate paths.

Facet is ecstatic, skipping down the road with Compass. Enthusiastic, non-stop chatter fills the air as the coblyn's thoughts flit fast, connecting new sights with known ideas, and commenting on the wonders of the land. Compass basks in the company and bounces jauntily along. Leaves crunch and twigs snap under their feet, birds sing nearby, and squirrels chatter from the trees. As the two friends walk and talk, Facet feels mental gears turning smoothly, thoughts sparking brightly. Everything encountered along their path seems to remind the coblyn of memories, stories, and ideas. Over several days, Compass notices how objects Facet knows seem to connect to memories easier and faster.

The two friends forage as they go, although Facet tends to collect more rocks and stones than edible items. While the coblyn finds any number of interesting wulfenite, iris agate, sodalite, tourmaline, hessonite, chrysocolla, and limonite, the duo only spots a few ripe elderberries and a handful of pecans at first; they avoid the wild carrot, as Facet remembers enough from Tonic to know there are some dangerous look-alikes, but not enough to properly verify its edibility. Fortunately, Compass has some good provisions packed, and is better at finding food than Facet is. The twin is able to find some wild blueberries, walnuts, and sweet potatoes. When food is low, Compass sometimes leads them off of their path for a detour to a town or village. The Night Tent is extremely useful for the duo's safe and comfortable sleeping. The joint missing the star, from when Facet sacrificed it for the Season Knights, slowly becomes less stable. "I'm going to need to fix that," Facet mentions, "so I hope we can find some Bits and Pieces."

One cold late-Autumn day, Compass inquires, "Facet, have you tried storing memories in items? I've noticed you have an easier time recalling things when you see an object that is attached to the memory. And I remember once meeting a spriggan who kept many things, because each was attached to a memory. Or was it a kobold? Well, no matter. Either way, their home was a kind of Museum, or a Nicknackatory of their memories."

Facet's eyes open wide with astonishment, "I could use items to store memories? What a splendid idea! I have been trying to figure out how to organize my thoughts ever since I returned from Mythwold." Remembering Nightshade's Knickknackatory the coblyn continues, "Of course, it might be harder to travel once I have lots of memory items. But there is lots I remember even without items, too. I remember basics, like walking and talking, stuff I use all the time; and I remember whatever is most recent. I need to write this down!" Facet stops for several minutes to write these ideas in the birchbark journal, then thanks Compass with a hug. Excited by this new find, Facet makes a conscious decision to keep items from important events. When the coblyn gets ready to walk again, there is a Bit! Shining right at the friends' feet. "Halfway there, Tent!" Facet crows with enthusiasm. Feeling ebullient, Facet does a hop-skip while tucking away the Bit.

The two continue their happy trails, and Facet practices recalling memories and facts both with and without memory items; memorabilia, as it were. The practice is rather stunted by the fact that there are not *very* many new items to keep for memories along this one path. The exercise is still fun for both Compass and Facet, who are enjoying the brisk days in their coats, and glad for the warmth inside the Night Tent when they sleep.

Chapter 29: Down When Up

On Overmorrow, Tonic and Weathervane hoist sails, heat the air, and fly up into the sky. They sail in peaceful, comfortable silence for a long while, enjoying the serenity of the bright, shining clear late-Autumn sky. Late in the day, they each have an apple, and roast up two water lily roots for their meal. The day is long and languid, quiet and cool. Tonic enjoys the freedom of knowing Weathervane is in charge, and that they are heading home. Days go by, much the same; Tonic finds the basket of the balloon to be cozy at first, but over time it becomes cramped and constricting to the tea gnome. The sky eventually seems bleak, no matter how colorful the sunset, nor how interesting the cloudscape, and Tonic starts to worry they aren't actually getting any closer to home. But the gnome of tea keeps these thoughts inside, so as not to worry Weathervane, nor seem ungrateful. The moth toy is always in the gnome's hand or front pocket. Tonic tries to decide whether to call it "Snug" or "Cordial."

Several more days and brief stops on the ground later, Tonic and Weathervane are floating across the sky in Overmorrow once again. As the beautiful skyscape lights the world, Tonic slumps down, squeezing the little moth toy from River Brindle. The gnome silently lets fat tears spatter on the floor from persimmon-orange eyes. The balloon continues on through the bright and breezy skies. A kaleidoscope of butterflies bursts forth from the trees below, and flutters past the balloon with the force of a sneeze on the breeze. Weathervane finishes tacking the sail and asks, "Dear friend, are you okay?"

Tonic's head shakes 'no' and the gnome breathes in shakily, "It's just…" Tonic sniffles, as a soft wind brushes a cheek, "It started out as a grand adventure, but some unexpected things happened and I feel stuck! I mean, I started because I feel stagnant at home, but this is more adventure than I wanted. I just needed a refresh! Instead I broke two cups, Briny got hurt. We can't seem to get home, and it is no longer fun. And this journey; I truly appreciate you, your friendship, your help. But this isn't *home*. I miss having a home, a place to play and visit friends, a garden for games, sharing scones and tea. Overmorrow's basket is too small for me. We've no outdoor space to call our own. We have no space to play games, or do art, or even just put chairs outside to sit. The Night Tent is no better; it's only big enough to sleep in, and it's made to be temporary. It's fine when traveling, but it isn't my *home*! Where's my Maplestump Mortar? My gardens? My Bramble? We are far from our friends, but even if they could get to us, there is not enough space to visit and play. I'm just so sad, and I want to go home." After a brief pause, the gnome continues, "And the worst part is that I know it isn't reasonable or fair;

I mean, we *found* Graemes, so we completed *my* quest, you are *helping* us all get home, Briny is even excited to be out in Mythwold, but... I *still* just really want to be *home*."

Weathervane heaves an understanding sigh and sits beside the tea gnome, "Good...it's good to give yourself space to be sad. Sometimes things happen that make us sad, or angry, or otherwise unhappy, and we need to feel that. Our bodies and brains need to process all our feelings. But what do you do once you're done being sad?"

Tonic shudders and sobs a bit longer, before answering. "You... do something? Like, you do something to fix what's wrong?" the gnome suggests tearfully.

"Yes," Weathervane encourages, "You have to find the next step, to do whatever the next thing that seems right is."

Tonic uses a sleeve and wipes away some tears, and a warm breeze dries them up. "But how long do you give yourself to be sad? How long do you get to just feel awful? How do you know when you are done, and when you are just wallowing beyond what's healthy?" Then Tonic gulps and cries a bit more, petting the plush moth.

Weathervane takes time to let the gnome cry before giving a (hopefully comforting) answer, "That's hard to say, Tonic. Different things need different amounts of time. And different beings react differently. I sometimes try to write my feelings out; I've started a lot of journals and poems."

Tonic looks up with despair, "So... you should feel unpleasant feelings, and at some point you should be done, but no one knows when, and you eventually will need to move on. Is that right?" Gentle zephyrs nudge Tonic's hands, and bounce against the two hair puffs.

Giving a light hug, Weathervane agrees, "Yeah. Basically, yes. Not very specific, I know, but true. You have said you want to be home. What defines home for you?"

"Home...It's where I *belong*. It's my sweet, ceramic

teapot house, my gardens with Bramble keeping watch, my Maplestump Mortar, and my two cauldrons by the door! It's where all my tools are, and everything is organized how I like it, and where I know my friends are nearby. Where I have my routine, and room to be creative; where everything is *comfy*." Tonic burbles.

Weathervane gives a sorrowful nod and an understanding squeeze to Tonic. "Maybe try focusing on that and the fact that we are headed towards it. I'm going to steer Overmorrow for a bit. I'm here."

Tonic steeps in sorrow for some time, slowly slipping into sleep, still hugging the soft moth toy. "Cordial, I think I've learned that I like *small* adventures, and that I really *dislike* change." Tonic murmurs to the plush moth.

Chapter 30: Quickly

The next day Tonic feels better, but nothing like fully restored. At Tonic's request, Weathervane monologues idly about many things, not expecting the tea gnome to join in. Tonic helps out with whatever Weathervane and Overmorrow need, including spotting an orchard to land in for gathering provisions. The gnome nuzzles Cordial, then tucks the toy securely into a petal pocket.

Once they've safely landed Overmorrow, the two friends spread out a bit; Tonic finds peaches and pears by following a strong waft of sweetness, while Weathervane discovers a grove of pecans. They are in the middle of gathering their delicious treasures, when an angry shout rings across the orchard.

A farmer with long, grassy fur lopes toward Tonic and Weathervane, growling and shouting at the two intruders.

Tonic and Weathervane walk toward the farmer, to try to apologize for the accidental theft, but are brought up short by the farmer's outraged tirade. The two friends stutter and stammer, trying to interject apologies while the farmer rants; Tonic is meek and worried, and Weathervane remains unabashed and straightforward.

The farmer's vituperation continues in an angry blur, covering everything from trespassers to honest landowners, laziness to hard work, sowing and reaping to begging for handouts, and oppression, sleazy travelers stealing jobs, the difficulty of growing a good crop, creatures feeling owed something they aren't, and how no one is willing to help a neighbor in trouble anymore, and finally finishing with, "Get off my patch and back to where you belong!"

Tonic has already backed up several steps to get away from the farmer's pruning shears which have been waved around during the long litany of gripes. Weathervane prudently nods concession to the grass-covered farmer, and firmly steers Tonic out of the orchard. Tonic tries to turn around, protesting, "I just want to pay for the fruits we collected!" when a clod of dirt smacks right into the side of the gnome's head; gravel-y chunks leave scrapes across Tonic's face, and fine sand particles slam into the gnome's ear. Weathervane's feathers provide some protection from the dirt missiles, but when Weathervane raises an arm to ward off the dirt clods, the farmer's pruning shears bludgeon into their arm with a nasty *thwack*.

With Tonic's left ear ringing from impact and face oozing blood, and Weathervane's right arm currently numb and useless, the two rush back to their balloon with alacrity.

Back at Overmorrow the friends quickly climb in, and Tonic, out of breath from their swift retreat, is pleased they at least have the fruit they picked. "I would have paid if the farmer had simply stopped yelling long enough." the gnome puffs.

"Yes, well," Weathervane responds drily, "some people on the path of life are friends, and some are not. Some are so unfriendly they don't even let you be civil. It was clear we weren't welcome there, and staying was not in the interests of our best health, even to pay for the items we had." As Weathervane and Tonic busy themselves with gears and heat and pulleys, Overmorrow lifts up into the sky.

Tonic thinks over the beings they've met since the Conclusions so long ago. "I'm really glad I met you and all the other kind friends on this journey, and that I haven't run afoul of many other unpleasant beings." With this thought, the gnome of tea, who is so far from home, begins to write some cards, filling them with thanks and doodles and joy and tales of travels, then folding them into whirligigs. Overmorrow floats sedately through the skies while tree jellies wave gelatinously from the woods below.

Chapter 31: Silvercatch

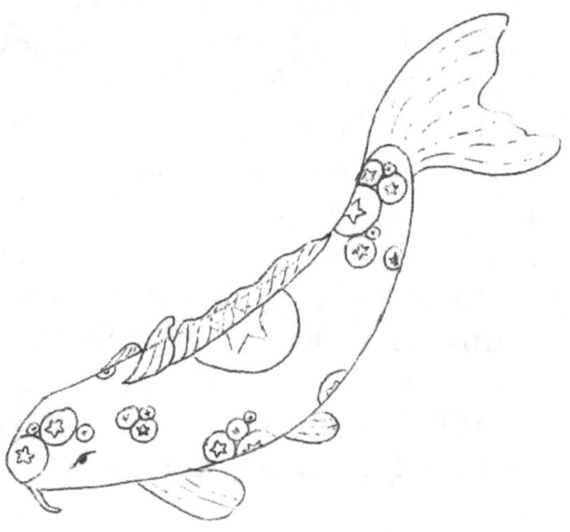

At their next landing, Weathervane, Compass, Tonic, and Facet all meet up just outside a busy town with a shimmering tower at the center. The mini-metropolis has a thriving river for trade and entertainment, large, well-traveled roads, and clean walls and latticed gates.

Facet's silvery-green eyes are wide as the coblyn tries to sort out and remember all of the sights, sounds, and smells of Thetower Town. "Is it a festival of some kind?" the coblyn asks, "There are so many bright flags up, and even from out here the noise is impressive!"

"Oh no," chuckles Compass, "It's just how Thetower is. Towns are quite big, and this one I think really ought to be updated to the name of *city*; it's been growing a lot! I'll mention it to the Classifiers."

Weathervane continues the explanation, "The big tower in the center has been here since before any other buildings; and being so conveniently near the river and at the intersection of several roads, people would plan to meet, buy, sell, and trade at "the tower." When the village first started to grow around that central feature, the name just stuck. And now the community has grown from a little village to a hectic city-size."

The group walks into the town, planning to buy some breakfast and other provisions. Thetower does, indeed, have bright flag-bunting up, just like the friends saw from over the stone wall outside the town, as well as beings *everywhere*, laughing, walking, arguing, eating, conversing, and selling wares. There are white buildings with dark brown wood beams, intricately carved shutters and porch lattices, beautiful little gardens, and ponds, fountains, and tiny streams all over. Watching a pond, Facet notices metallic glimmers in the water. "Is that a wishing pond?" the coblyn asks, while going over to look.

"Oh, I think you may have spotted a koin!" Compass answers enthusiastically.

"Well, coins *are* what you usually throw into water to make a wish." says Facet with some confusion.

Compass looks bothered for a moment, then brightens, "No, no; a *koin*! They are a type of fish made of living metal; koins are revered here, and the major cause of Thetower's continued success. The koins originally lived wild in the natural ponds nearby, but now there is a thriving community in the town's fountains and streams too. It is very good luck to see one! Sometimes they even grant wishes. Apparently it evolved as some sort of self-defense to stop fishers from catching and eating them."

Facet walks over to a pond and peers in, trying to spot an elusive koin. The coblyn adjusts the goggles to keep their quartz hair out of the way.

Weathervane adds, "Apparently Thetower's ruler, Silvercatch, was the one who cared for and tended the wild koins, and who eventually brought some to live in the town."

Tonic is startled, and says with awe, "Silvercatch Loques? Really?! But Silvercatch is *famous*; the Keeper of Secrets, the Last Challenge! They say Silvercatch connects all locked and forgotten places, and wears liquid silver that reflects the truth of any matter. Silvercatch, it is said, is hardly ever seen, preferring to remain with the secrets and forgotten places."

Weathervane nods and points, "Yes, and lives in a tower of packed snow. That one, in the middle of the town you are currently standing in!"

Tonic gapes at the tower, marveling at the knowledge that such a legend really exists, "But, wait. How would anyone even know if the Keeper of Secrets is really in the tower? Silvercatch is only supposed to appear as a last challenge to a locked and forgotten place of secrets. Surely those don't happen that often?"

A vendor nearby starts calling to the group, hawking their wares. Compass and Weathervane look up at the shimmering tower.

"And how would a tower of packed snow survive the summer sun?" Tonic continues.

More townsfolk grumpily break into the conversation, trying to sell, buy, or just persuade the trio to be interested in various merchandise.

Nearby, Facet is watching the pond. A silver koin with dark copper spots flicks a fin as Facet gazes, and the coblyn realizes there are many koins in the pond, all sorts of shimmery metallic colors; gold, silver, copper, platinum, black, bronze, iron... Each beautiful koin swims around slowly, languorously. They mostly stay in the shade, which makes them hard to notice, but sometimes one will dart out into sunny waters, like a shining streak beneath the water. The koins are so fast it is hard to prove, even to yourself, that you really saw one; perhaps it was just the glint of sunlight? Watching carefully, Facet notices that every koin fish has at least two colors. The speckles and splotches on the koins seem to be regular in pattern. After more quiet observation and sketching, the coblyn realizes the spots on the fish are basically circle shapes, each with a tiny central color in the shape of a star, key, lock, or smaller circle. Facet dips a finger in the water, and after a few slow moments pass, a bold brass koin flashes by, kissing the coblyn's knuckle and leaving a shiny key image there.

A loud trumpeting sound breaks Facet's concentration, and looking around the coblyn notices that Tonic, Weathervane, and Compass are all gone. Everyone seems to be looking toward the tower, where tiny cloth wings flutter out of a high window. Another movement catches Facet's eye, and the coblyn hurries over to the gate, scooting outside Thetower town, and catching up with the three hurrying friends.

"Good to have you Facet!" Compass says. "Best we were out of there."

Weathervane agrees, puffing, "The locals did not like our thinking too much about their tower or Silvercatch. They were getting...upset, with our conversation."

Quickening their pace, they hurry away from Thetower and the coblyn is unable to tell them about the fish. After a bit, the group slows as they approach Overmorrow and Facet is able to blurt out, "I got kissed by a koin!" showing off the marked knuckle Facet continues, "it left a lovely image, just like a tiny key."

"That is said to be bracingly lucky!" Weathervane breathes, "May it bring you fairwinds in all things."

"But now," Compass adds, "let us all get to the trails, in case the townsfolk decide we need a sterner lesson about their ideals."

With that, the group splits up, Tonic and Weathervane to the sky, and Compass and Facet to the roads, but all heading swiftly away from Thetower.

Chapter 32: Season's Shores

In Overmorrow, Tonic takes out the colored papers from Vellum and writes letters to all the beings they've met on their travels: beings from here in Fierlund, from the mythical Mythwold, every name that can be remembered is put neatly on a list, and checked off as the letter is written. The garden gnome folds each letter and adds them to the whirly-gig-ed notes from earlier. Somewhere in the middle of writing, Tonic is thinking and patting Cordial the plushy moth, and remembers Wynn's advice to enjoy the memories when you are done traveling. Pondering this, the gnome of tea carefully uses a few sheets to write down stories of the journey, and tucks them into Curious Rituals for safekeeping.

Weathervane and Tonic sail through vast cloudscapes and vibrant sunsets, over lakes, cities, forests, towns, mountains, villages, deserts, and fields. The season gets colder, and nudges into winter. Tonic introduces Weathervane to all sorts of plants when they are on the ground: different trees, flowers, roots, and all their names and uses. There are small adventures foraging ingredients, cooking meals, buying provisions, traversing storms, and generally getting closer and closer to the Seasons' Shores. Throughout, Tonic drops finished whirligig letters toward Vellum and the Librarians in the Ideas Orchard, Mushroom the unicorn, Nightshade in the Epicerie Forest, River Brindle in the Twisting Village, Notyet at the Snail's Gift, Driftwood in Castledom, Petrichor and Wynn and Briny and Graemes in Mythwold, and Clover and Bramble back home, asking Steam to deliver each of them safely.

Compass and Facet walk along slightly slower, but have an easier time finding shelter during storms, and hardly ever worry about being blown down out of the sky. The two travel companions discuss modes of travel, different cuisine, types of landscape, life philosophy, and how to find a proper star gear to fix the NightTent (which has started to let in a blustery winter breeze when it is set up). There are manybeings to chat with, and wonderful stones, earths, caves, grottos, and bogs to interest Facet. The coblyn makes several mud paintings of the landscapes they see, collecting different colors and ochres as they find them, to add to the palette jars. Facet frequently remarks on unusual features: a bright whirligig seed racing by overhead, a unique frog song, jack'o'lantern mushrooms, and other interesting tidbits that catch the coblyn's attention along the way.

Finally Weathervane lands Overmorrow on the sandy beach of Season's Shores. From above the landscape is unfamiliar, but as they touchdown Tonic realizes that this is where the mountain and the Season Knights used to be! The tea gnome strolls around, reminiscing about the long-ago start of their adventure; although Tonic starts to grouse, questions from Weathervane reveal a story of how friendship, teamwork, and perseverance helped Tonic, Briny, and Facet through the tough times, and added extra joy to their trip.

"Where are you heading next?" Tonic asks Weathervane. "You have been so much help getting us home, and I would like to help you in return. Is there anything you need for provisions?"

"Having your company was a delightful change to my usual travels, Tonic! And of course, I've so many new stories for me and Compass. What do you recommend by way of beach-ly provisions?"

When Facet and Compass arrive a goodly while later, they find a small shelter and a much grander stage constructed on the beach. Weathervane has a collection of seaside snacks stored in the shelter, and gnome and Nightjar are making signs to direct travelers toward the "Twins Story Stage (at Seasons' Shore)!" Delighted with the idea, Compass and Facet begin helping too.

Compass marks the trail, clearing it and putting up signs towards the "Seemers Extrodinaire!" Facet builds lights, using a newly-found Sudden Idea (which lights up under its black wings with a pale yellow stripe) to assist, and attaching some to the stage and some to the trail signs. Facet and the trusty Maplet work out the best positioning of stage, seats, and other spatial things. Tonic and Weathervane work on painting and sewing, and moving things around to Facet's instructions.

Tonic does some foraging and is able to make several new herbal shoreline tisanes using coconut, serviceberry, hibiscus, beach strawberry, pea flower, beach plum, and blackberry. The gnome collects fresh cool stream water in a large glass carafe and steeps the tisane blends in the sunlight, creating refreshing sips for the group. The pieces are getting finished, and over the course of a few days other beings begin to show up. The signs help spread the word about the twin story-tellers' stage.

Eventually the stage is all set up, beings are arriving to experience the Nightjar twins' stories, and somebeings are even setting up small stalls to sell hats, meals, drinks, and art.

Tonic and Facet stay to watch several shows and serve snacks to everybeing, making some good deals and trades. They also build another spot just to make and serve refreshments for the shows. The Nightjar Twins are well set-up and both are enjoying their place on the shore. After several suns have risen and set, Tonic starts to feel anxious for home again. As much as the tea garden gnome enjoys work helping others, the urge to return home is stronger.

Facet and Tonic decide to pack up their things and continue heading for home. They take a route marked for them by Weathervane, who found it by using the Useful Far-seeing Device while up in Overmorrow. As they get closer to where they once began, the two friends wonder, after such a long journey, "What is home going to be like?"

Chapter 33: New Beginnings

Facet finds a Hop Stop and the duo use some of the Beans they earned selling food and drinks at the Season's Shore to rent Hopper Carts. With the days getting chilly, Tonic and Facet put on their heavier coats before zooming away. The path back to the friends' homes is quicker than their journey out was. The Hopper Carts go faster and the route is more direct. They chat and sing, and Tonic starts to feel giddy, both happy and anxious, about getting home. Facet enjoys the ride, watching the hills zip by and enjoying the bumps and dips on the path. The Night Tent continues to be a comfort whenever they need to sleep on their travels. Sooner than Facet expected, the friends split up to head to their separate homes.

Tonic's pace quickens as wafts of tea, cinnamon, sage, and pine puff down the path. Soon the gnome sees the cinnamon tree out front and gives a small whoop, "Home!" The garden looks a bit higgledy piggledy, but the ceramic teapot still looks bright and inviting. The stone bench and wood table remain in the front garden, and Tonic waves to the stream along the house's handle-side. Even from here, the gnome knows the cauldrons need cleaning, and sees the Maplestump Mortar has small sprouts growing on it. The Scrubby Bubbleup will be so useful to clean out the cauldrons! With a small sneeze and a hug to the cinnamon tree, Tonic holds out a hand to pet the tea plants while carefully picking a way down the overgrown path; every bush is full and hale. "Greetings and hospitality, Bramble!" the gnome sneezes and kneels down by the blackberry, "I see you've kept watch over the tea gardens, thank you. The bushes are all healthy and robust!"

Peeking around the back of the house, Tonic notices some grasses encroaching around the edges, and some of the plants are *quite* in need of trimming; we won't even *mention* the mint. The pines are springing up seedlings all over, the sage has burst out of its beds, while the lemon and elder are getting cramped by other plants. Orange, clove, and nutmeg seem to have joined forces against unwanted grasses and vines. Jasmine has taken over a patch of wooden fence and is fiercely holding its own against any invaders. There are also some wild Leaf Sheep grazing near the stream; they've clearly taken up residence, as Tonic sees rows of baby vegetable lambs growing at the edge of the garden.

The hickory hull door sticks a bit, but with an extra whack from the Mighty Teaspoon Hammer it finally opens. Inside, the teapot house is certainly dusty, there is a puddle from a leak in the roof, and the saucer-shaped windows are very grubby. The once-brightly colored cushions need refreshing, the books on the shelves need reading, and when Tonic sees a reflection, the gnome notes how their outfit's stitching needs fixing too. The gnome of tea chooses a ton of tea blends, puts the kettle on to boil, and gets out a broom to start sweeping. But first, Tonic gets out a fresh journal (a special cinnamon and birchbark journal acquired ages ago, then stored neatly among all the other patiently-waiting journals Tonic has) and starts writing down memories from the Wanderlust adventure to enjoy here at home, while Cordial sits on the table and watches. The gnome adds scraps to the book; drawings, colors, sketches, leaves and flowers all add visual details and textures to the written words. Tonic titles the journal, "Conclusions to Beginnings." There is a lot to do: many cozy, close-by adventures to have, and it is so good to be home.

Facet's cave full of tidy-piles is still in its usual hill, but the path and hill are both tangly and overgrown. One of the colored-jewel windows has a chip in it, and there is a foam of Clickfish living on the hill; the grasses and flowers glisten with soaps. Looking over the Gem Basin, the coblyn sees soap dried between the crystal shards, and knows the Gem Basin has been useful to the migrating Clickfish. Listening to their clicking, Facet wonders if this is the foam who has always lived here at homecave, or if it is a new, wild group of click fish.

Inside the cave, the kitchen still has all the usual iron kettles and copper pots, but the cave is no longer full of cozy glows. Dirt and leaves have blown in through the cracked window, coating things in grime; there's an Idle Notion sleeping by the hearth.

Looking around at the overwhelming list of things to do, Facet's mind jumps to a million more ideas. The coblyn fumbles out the trusty (and now more-than-slightly tattered) birchbark journal, "Nearly full. I'll have to fix that too." and hurries to write down all the fleeting thoughts. "New birchbark pages? journal?, adventures?, What about the koin kiss?, I might be a Dabbler or maybe a Seemer?, fix pane - new jewels, move Clickfish, rinse soaps, clean house, sweep, scrub, dishes, dust, new broom?, Turbine go?, exercise Idle Notion, trim path, weed meadow, repair gloves, check for Clickfish or blue glaucus dragons in the water…”

Overwhelmed by the list and unable to decide where to start, Facet shakes out a blanket and curls up to take a nap. Everything will need to get done, but it will have to wait; there is too much to do, and the coblyn hopes it will seem less overwhelming after a nap. Trying to drift off, the coblyn’s thoughts spin, and Facet wonders if even the hard packed dirt, earthenware bowls, metal, and stone of the house will be enough to keep a solid grounding of thought now. “Oh yes,” the coblyn writes another note, “build Knicknackatory.”

Fierlund’s seasons turn, from frosts to buds to copper-colored skies. The leafsheep thrive, the clickfish bubble, Clover visits, a bob of selkies move into Briney’s sandcastle; the selkies eventually move on, and since neither sandcastle nor shipwreck is prized for their staying power when left unattended, the ocean continues reclaiming that house and redistributing its pieces. Facet and Tonic cannot tell for sure if Steam and Turbine are around, but sometimes it seems like the wind is extra sweet and playful.

Facet tends to the Idle Notion for a while, until it trundles further into the cave. Facet also cares for the Sudden Ideas, tidies the beloved piles system of organization, collects memories for the newly-built Knicknackatory, and befriends the foam of Clickfish. True to coblyn nature many things are planned, invented, and intended, and a portion even come to fruition. The coblyn masters the multitool from Mythwold, and devises some new devices with it. Facet’s favorite creation is a necklace they made to remember the friends’ journey; the necklace has a labradorite cabochon for Facet, a metal tea leaf for Tonic, and a wire-wrapped pearl for Briny. Facet also tries to write notes to friends regularly, but always gets distracted by other things, so missives happen only sporadically.

Tonic applies to be a Steeper at the Samovar, and while awaiting a reply, the tea gnome keeps writing letters to friends from afar and even gets several back in return. WindRabbit Couriers are renowned for their swift delivery and Tonic likes to think that Steam *is* around and couriers the correspondences. The gnome enjoys both sending and receiving notes penned with pals, and delights in decorating the papers and envelopes with sketches, colors, and doodles.

Vellum writes back, in a neat, precise script, and Grotto often includes some notes too; their notes generally have fascinating little paper pockets and pop-ups as well. Driftwood sends missives with extra trinkets like charms, flowers, crumbs, etc., and Facet loves reading (and explaining) them to Tonic; the rusalka seems to think in similar ways as the coblyn, and their non sequiturs are less nonsensical to each other. Both coblyn and gnome enjoy the updates and stories from friends.

One lazy late-summer day Facet and Tonic are visiting and tending to the gnome's now-tamed flock of leaf sheep. Tonic is just voicing a wish to build a new space for the leaf sheep when there is a wind with the hint of icy weather on the horizon. A bright rectangle with about a hundred tiny pictures on it floats, flips, tumbles, and flops down in the garden between coblyn and gnome; the paper smells of salt and ozone. The two friends stare at the envelope in bafflement until a leaf sheep tries to eat it.

Swiping the letter off the ground (almost bumping heads in their haste), Facet and Tonic examine it: there are many tiny pictures glued on the top right corner, the shimmering blue ink in the center reads "Tonic and Facet, the Meadows, Teapot or Cave" and there is a smear of gel ink imprinted on it in the image of a racing snail that says "Snail Mail" stamped across the top of three of the glued-on pictures. With wonder, coblyn and gnome open the envelope and the two begin to read:

"Facet and Tonic, my dear friends,
I hope this letter finds you well. Graemes and I have been exploring Mythwold, and is it ever amazing! I still can't use my legs very long, but I now have a magic chair to help me; it runs on Eel Tricks! (I have never seen the eels, though. Apparently they are very tiny, and travel by lightning!) We made it to the Sydney Opera House *ages* ago, and explored all over; it was amazing! Big, and bright, and white, and with *beautiful*, stunning performances inside! But since Villepreux isn't a living creature here, we took lots of notes and magic sketches called photographs to show her later. The pirates were a problem, but we are fine; it's really the Bermuda sirens you need to be careful of. Also, I asked Spindrift to go back and deliver this letter, so I really hope that worked! I wrote the ink with my WindRabbit pen, then mailed it with stamps from the Post Office here, then put it Somewhere Safe (which Graemes says is the only magic spell of ours that seems to work in Mythwold. It ensures the item gets lost. Which I'm hoping combined with my WindRabbit ink will get this letter to you!). *Did* this letter get to you? I got your letters, but I keep forgetting to write. Until now, clearly. Keep the kettle warm for me, okay? We will be back soon!
Smooth sailing,
Briny"

Facet does a jumpy jig with the letter, while Tonic swirls around and hugs trees in joy, both thinking of their good friends off traveling in the World of Myth. Tonic tucks the letter tidily into the cinno-birch bark journal of the friends' traveling tales for safe-keeping.

Later that evening, after much discussion about Briny's note, Facet is getting ready to head back to their home cave. The two friends have trimmed tea bushes ("same old bushes" thinks Tonic), brushed leaf sheep (always so tangled), pruned plants (again), weeded the garden (the usual weeds), and cleaned up the paths (weren't these swept just yesterday?).

Gnome and coblyn are pleased with the work and nicely tired at the end of the day. They are finishing sharing a pot of tea, and Facet is just putting away cleaned cups to dry. Tonic rustles around the teapot home for a while, anxious and grumpy. "The house is too small. The gardens never change. Everything is so cramped. Facet, I can't stand it anymore! I need a new house." The gnome bursts out.

Facet blinks slowly and responds, "Are you sure, Tonic? You hate learning new routines, and you didn't enjoy our last adventure very much while we were on it."

"But that was just about finding Graemes. This is about needing a whole new house! I can't properly do any weaving in here, and my kitchen is too dirty, and the laundry is impossible to keep up with, and I never feel 'outside' enough when I'm inside. I need more space!" The gnome replies with frustration, as a gentle shimmery lustre curls through the air.

"Tonic, for a gnome who is a self-declared small-adventures-only being, you seem to attract a lot of Wanderlusts." Facet chuckles, watching the shimmer. "What if we built you a good sunroom porch for more "outside" feeling when you are inside? Would that help?"

Tonic's nose wrinkles in thought and the gnome replies with a sigh, "No."

Facet looks around the mostly tidy, well-organized

ceramic teapot home: the carefully collected teacups, the dusted and sorted books, Bramble the blackberry plant waving in the breeze outside. Then the coblyn says with a reflective air, "Well, I'm quite tired tonight, however, we could certainly go tomorrow. You'll want something all-new, correct? No need to bother with the tedious packing and hauling; make a fresh start with all new things." Facet looks thoughtful and serious, then with a wave, the coblyn heads home, smiling.

Tonic's eyes get wide from feeling startled and upset at the suggestion. Leave *all* their things behind? But of course, the coblyn's suggestion makes sense... it's just that the chestnut burr cauldron is working so well, and the passionflower cauldron always steeps such delicate teas. A sunroom *would* be nice, but what about a bigger yard? And the pantry really is too small and in such an odd nook... then again, it took so long to grow the gardens this nicely... Tonic continues to putter around the house and fruitlessly debate what the best new house would be like until late in the evening. There is a faint clink outside as the evening mail is delivered. Eventually the garden gnome drifts off to sleep, dreaming of house possibilities and worrying over what to move.

Facet whistles on the way back to homecave, waving at a passing windrabbit Courier (who smells a bit like bog or sulfur, and is carrying a letter with the Samovar's stamp on it), fairly certain that a small adventure is all Tonic needs; perhaps the complexity of looking at new homes and planning for moving will be enough adventure for the tea garden gnome. Finding a new place is live is often exhausting, and the coblyn knows that their friend *hates* moving; from picking a place, to packing up, from the inevitable sacrifice of losing items, to the disappointment of a new place's difficulties and imperfections: Tonic hates it all.

Facet shakes their head, making long, quartz-y locks shimmer, and decides to see if Tonic wants to join the new tumbling and acrobatics studio over in the Heathers.

Once inside the inviting coppery-bronze homecave, Facet looks around and breathes a deep, contented inhale. Taking in the organizational piles, bright kitchen, scattered notes, possibility parts, inventions, and Sudden Ideas, the coblyn decides to try out being a Dabbler. Facet has a pleasant, fresh feeling of getting to focus on something new. Outside the clickfish quietly bubble around in the dusk breezes and invisible windrabbits frolic and tumble in rabbity games.

Back at the teapot, Tonic is busily adding ideas to the cinno-birch bark journal, and embellishing sketches to their stories. The journal is already becoming well-loved and well-worn as the tea gnome frequently leafs through the pages, adding thoughts and reflections and re-reading the journey. Conclusions to Beginnings has many more pages in it, just ready for more adventurous memories. Tonic has already added some notes about what makes a perfect house.

So you see, this is just a perfectly ordinary story, about an everyday adventure, from Fierlund to Mythwold and home.

The Characters:

Clover Miel

A pooka. Pookas are known for their ties to animals; some say pookas have the ability to shapeshift into the animals they are most like, although no one has ever seen Clover do this. Most pookas love nature and enjoy spending quiet time with animals; in fact, pookas often prefer animal friends over friendships with otherbeings. Clover is especially skilled in baking, honey, pollinators, and flowers. This pooka smells of clover, peach, and orange blossoms, and wears a mix of black and vibrant floral shades. Clover is short and furry of stature, with black, spikey hair containing yellow streaks; this pooka uses their hands to speak. Always has an oakcorn bucket. Nectar-yellow eyes. High energy. Is a traveler who works with the Apis Distillery and Bloomiery. Travelers often have bright, intricate handcarts full of stories and supplies; Clover's handcart is mostly bright yellow and cool grey, with geometric woodwork patterns all over it.

Tonic Cuppa

A garden gnome of tea. Gnomes tend to excel at plant-based skills, like botany, herbology, whittling, basket weaving, etc. Like most gnomes, Tonic is usually a bit smudged from gardening, and loves a good hike. Gnomes are hard workers, and they love a tidy space. Tonic's specialty is gardening and blending teas. Wields the Mighty Teaspoon Hammer, and often uses it as a walking stick, shovel, and general solution; wears it slung across the back when not in use. Smells of all things tea; the fresh of mint, bergamot, and orange, the warmth of cinnamon, nutmeg and clove, and the uplifting of jasmine and peach blossoms. Wears sturdy

clothing of greens and browns (pale sage to shady forest,
and creamy birch to rich cocoa) with bright embroidery
designs. Wears green-tipped curly brown hair up in 2 puffs.
Moss-dappled bark skin. Persimmon orange eyes. Carries a
peach pack with snacks and sips inside. Has a travel teapot
for Steam the windrabbit. Nose crinkles when thinking
hard. Pats their hair puffs or rubs their moss patches when
nervous. Lives in a teapot; house is clean and the many items
Tonic has are all stowed and organized. Teapot is pretty
small because most of the gnome's time is spent outside
(gardening, walking, caring for plants, grinding herbs, etc).

Windrabbit Steam

A zephyr caught for Tonic by Briny; Zephyrs are playful,
friendly windrabbits. Steam looks like faint green and brown
curls of sweetly-scented tea. Wears a ceramic collar which
allows anybeing to see it. The collar has a tiny teacup charm,
and a teabag tag with Steam's name on it.

Facet Cabochon

A coblyn of earth and stone. Coblyns are generally
interested in tinkering, collecting stuff, and are excellent
at noticing disregarded objects (which often turn out to
be Bits, Pieces, and Sudden Ideas); they also often need to
write notes and sketch ideas, so they like to keep journals
(birchbark for preference) though some coblyns collect far
more journals than they use. Coblyns enjoy earthy things
such as being bare-footed, painting, making pottery, and
exploring caves. Facet's specialty is inventing and lapidary;
cannot help but design and create; excitable and slightly
clumsy. Smells of coppery metal and cool stones. Skin is
the variegated colors of earth, with jade highlights. Wears
an amethyst purple and citrine yellow Stratigraphy Skirt.
Favors gold, bismuth, and iolite jewelry. Long, quartzey hair

has amethyst clusters in it, and is kept tied back with willow reeds and grape vine. Silvery grey eyes with a lustrous green patina. Always has a belt of tools and a birchbark journal. A few wires and stones remain within reach, and collections of spare Possibility Parts stick out of the belt's pockets. Bronze bag for any interesting items found. Fingers twist, sift, and crinkle objects when nervous. Facet lives in a sprawling cave full of many parts, items, and interesting trinkets. As with many coblyns, Facet tries to be organized, but quickly reverts to the "piles" method of organizing; still usually able to find items in their own piles, so long as no one has touched them.

Windrabbit Turbine

This windrabbit is Facet's friend. This playful Zephyr type windrabbit looks like a shifting, sparkling, mineral mist. Turbine wears a braided metal collar, which has a 'Turbine' tag just above a gear pendant.

Briny Nimbus

A water and weather sprite. Most sprites enjoy cloud watching, camping, exploring, swimming, and visiting new places; they also tend to be very energetic and enjoy visiting everybeing! Briny's specialty is ocean and rain. Smells of saltwater and ozone. Wears all shades of blue (from light rain to deep ocean) in flowing outfits. Likes hints of rainbows in accessories. Has a windrabbit that can only be seen by other creatures with water-sight, until a special collar is made. Briny has short, wavy hair the blue-grey of storms, ice blue eyes, Briny's skin is the light creamy-white color of frothy waves, until during the story it changes to be dark like river stones and angry tide pools. Uses a seafoam satchel to carry necessities. Eyes flash like lightning when startled or angry, flips and sprays hair when nervous. Briny lives in a small shipwreck and sandcastle; the walls above the sea are made of a sand, glass, and seashell mixture called tabby, there are windows and skylights in abundance, and the part under the waves is shipwreck; it is all very sparse and tidy. The sprite doesn't keep or collect very many things, new items arrive on the tide to be decorations for a day or two, then are washed away again into the sea.

Windrabbit Spindrift

A gale type windrabbit. This is Briny's windrabbit, and it shimmers like the rainbow reflection of wind. Spindrift bounces like bubbles, and enjoys causing light mischief, kicking up air and splashing flecks of water around.

Nightshade

A dryad who lives in the Epicerie Forest. A friend of Graemes's; they once worked together on cleaning up a nasty gingerbread curse.

Vellum

Librarian in the Ideas Orchard. Has pale skin and short white hair, with multitudes of inks stained onto fingers. Berry-bright leather journal for notes. Smells of rosewood and sandalwood. Wears a metal owl pendant.

Grotto

Has many freckles and a lush tumble of mahogany hair in many braids. Warm smile and hickory-grain eyes. Assistant Librarian at the Ideas Orchard.

River Brindle

A villager from the Village of Twist. River Brindle is tall and lithe, with large hazel eyes, beautiful wavy orange hair, and black stripes from cat-like ears to tail-tip. Wears small hoop earrings, a black vest, and brown pants. Helps Tonic through Twist Village.

Weathervane Poorwhill Nightjar

Actor and Explorer. Tonic, Briny, and Facet meet up with the Nightjar Twins as they approach the lintel to the World's Between. Weathervane is rather bird-like, with a small beak, and mottled brown, black, and cream colored feathers and skin. Weathervane wears spectacles and a light blue cravat, and rides in a brightly-colored hot air balloon-ship called Overmorrow. Outgoing and enthusiastic. Lost a beloved moonstone necklace. Uses the greeting "Fair winds!"

Compass Frogmouth Nightjar

One of the Nightjar Twins, Compass travels by land as the siblings explore and act out their discoveries. Always has pens and tins handy. Uses the greeting, "Clear trails!" Has a wide beak, and is mottled in brown, black, and cream. Wears a cable knit sweater and a sturdy backpack.

Notyet the Snail

Uses the greeting, "How's the road?" Owns the tavern/restaurant/inn called The Snail's Gift. Wears a sturdy yellow apron, neutral/pastel clothes, and large, rounded glasses. Probably a pooka. Has dark green eyes, and dark brown, teal, and white hair, usually pulled up in a shell-like swirling bun. Patient and kind, listens to travelers and gives advice.

Graemes

A friend and mentor of Tonic. She/her. Has traveled widely, and crossed the World's Between many times. Graemes has her peppery-white hair braided up in a bun, loose-fitting cotton overalls over a bright shirt, and oval glasses on her nose. Sails The Changing Wind across the World's Between with Villepreux.

Villepreux

A friend (and boat) of Graemes's. Began as a folded paper octopus in the Mythwold/World of Myth. Changed into a living paper nautilus the first time Graemes traveled the World's Between to Fierlund/Land of Legend. Wishes to see if the Sydney Opera House is actually an ancient nautilus.

Petrichor

Tylwyth Teg; from Fierlund, now lives in Mythwold. They/She/He. Does a lot of crafting of all kinds of plants. Has tattoos of crafts and plants on their arms, wears their wavy dyed-green-and-blue hair in a low ponytail. Also wears thrifted and handmade clothes with plant buttons, embroidery, and prints, and sturdy, dark boots. Probably about 25-30 years old.

Wynn

Friend of Petrichor. She/her. Is an EMT (Emergency Medical Technician). Always energetic, very caring and calm in chaotic situations. About 30 years old. Has short, curly brown hair. Unknown history.

Glossary:
(Facet's notes from Vellum)

Brindled – stripy (and sometimes also spotted) color pattern on a creature.

Biscuitroot – a plant that is tolerant to dry conditions; sometimes used as a starchy root vegetable

Bole – a sort of knot or bulge in the bark of a tree or large shrub.

Briny – word for water that is salty. The name of our sprite.

Coddiwomple – to travel purposefully to a vague destination, rather like a wanderlust.

Disgruntled – a mood or feeling, similar to unhappy or fussy.

Facet – word for a flat side of something, especially associated with cut gems. The name of our coblyn.

Fae – We have many words for these beings, in every culture here in Mythwold, including: faeries, fairies, fair folk, nisse, shining host, spirits, sidhe, yokai, etc.

Gnome – a being of what we call "fairies" generally associated with earth and gardens.

Coblyn – a being of what we call "fairies" generally associated with holes, caves, mosses, and often depicted with green skin.

Iolite – a type of stone. Translucent, many shifting colors inside it.

Lagomorph – word meaning, approximately, "of, about, or concerning rabbit-related creatures."

Lithe – a thin, athletic build.

Melancholy – feeling sad or upset.

Moderate – not too much, not too little of something. Can also mean to be a judge or neutral position between several opposing views.

Mottled – many colors or pieces squished together.

Pertinent – important or related to a thing.

Petrichor – the word for the smell after rain. The name of the tylwyth teg we meet in Mythwold; closely tied to plants and seasons.

Ploy – plan, scheme, feint.

Pooka – a being of what we call "fairies" generally associated with wild animals, shapeshifting, and mischief.

Quercus Alba – scientific name for a White Oak tree.

Regale – to tell a long, entertaining story.

Salsify – a plant in the dandelion family, sometimes used as a root vegetable.

Salutation – a greeting.

Sprite – a being of what we generally call "fairies" generally associated with one of the natural elements (earth, air, fire, water).

Tome – a large, old book.

Tonic – word for a curative or medicinal drink. The name of our tea gnome.

Trepidation – feeling of worry or unease.

Tylwyth Teg – a type of what we call "fairies," this word is used in Wales.

Urging – encouraging a being to do something.

Vellum – a fancy type of stiff, translucent paper.

Wanderlust – the need to travel, not necessarily to a specific destination.

Womble – a rumble in the tummy when you are hungry.

Who is the author?

Serella Savenko insists on being listed as "probably human," as "publishers refuse to make books cobbled together by a random stack of semi-mythical forest creatures in a jacket." It's likely best not to argue. This surprising collection of

atoms has been mucking about with both words and images, in a semi-formal way, since at least the middle grades. This author-illustrator has a Bachelor degree in Sociology, a minor in Philosophy, a Masters in Teaching, and has a bizarre collection of job experience including festival performer, state park ranger, scent alchemist, and a teacher from elementary to high school.

Savenko enjoys hunting down dopamine in a variety of areas, not limited to: sketching, puns, nature, painting, singing badly, reading, yarncrafts, tea, tiny things, origami, story telling, fresh baked bread, clay, geekery, jewelry-making, being cozy, good friends, and cool words like "lapidary." Savenko currently lives in the state of Mild Bewilderment at a house with a spouse, kids, garden, and cats.

If you enjoy such silliness, you can find more at:

https://www.LuckyPooka.com

https://www.Patreon.com/LuckyPooka